Talking with Boys is an astonishing story collection that spans decades and is set in various locales, including Houston, Lahore, and Dubai. With deep insight and humor, Tayyba Kanwal explores the diverse range of the Pakistani and Pakistani American experience, as well as the complexities of a Muslim identity. Readers are introduced to a big cast of rich and memorable characters, many of whom are navigating new beginnings and places. Whether writing about family dynamics, generational conflicts, immigration, socioeconomic class, and notions of home and belonging, among other themes, Kanwal's stories speak to the human condition with breathtaking power. A remarkable debut.

— GHASSAN ZEINEDDINE, author of *Dearborn*

An intimate collection of stories, *Talking with Boys* spans time and place while depicting a group of souls who are determined, hilarious, and complex. Kanwal knows this world better than anyone, which is why the collection is consistently full of provocation and delight. This book is the introduction of an exciting new literary voice that readers will be sure to enjoy.

— MAURICE CARLOS RUFFIN, author of *The American Daughters*

There is something wonderfully disarming about all the people in these stories. Kanwal narrates their lives in sentences that are poignant, their plans, faults and longing always at the center, their utter humanness laid out on the pages.

— FARAH ALI, author of *The River, The Town*

Talking with Boys is a magical and riveting collection that will make you reassess what you know about the three very different worlds in which the stories are set. Kanwal's agile, multifaceted characters are at once hilarious and heartbreaking. They'll shock you and infuriate you and amaze you. They'll linger in your imagination long after you've turned the last page.

— CHITRA DIVAKARUNI, American Book Award-winning author of *Independence* and *Mistress of Spices*

Tayyba Kanwal

Talking with Boys
stories

Black Lawrence Press

Black Lawrence Press

Executive Editor: Diane Goettel
Immigrant Writing Series Founder & Director: Abayomi Animashaun
Immigrant Writing Series Editors:
Ewa Chrusciel, Rigoberto González, 신 선 영 Sun Yung Shin
Book Cover Design: Zoe Norvell
Cover Art: "Quest" by Jan-Frits Obers
Book Interior Design: Serena Solin

ISBN: 9781625571793

Published 2026 by Black Lawrence Press.
Printed in the United States.

Contents

For Rashed, who saw the steel in the silk

The Girl Who Ran

Houston, 2015

Two weeks after she turned eighteen, Amal married Zee, the boy her family had forbidden her from seeing. Friday afternoon, he skipped classes at the university, picked her up from high school, and they raced off to the mosque—not the fussy one up in River Oaks, but one way down Bissonnet where the zip codes were still Houston, and the strip malls were no man's land.

In the back seat of Zee's BMW convertible, Amal dug out of her backpack a crumpled green silk kurta pajama, a gift from her unsuspecting Dadi, her grandmother who'd just flown in from Pakistan. Once they pulled onto the highway, Amal slid out of her school skirt to ease on the legging pants. "Eyes on the road," she warned Zee.

When her uniform polo came off, Zee blew her a kiss in the rearview mirror. Giggling, Amal clambered to the front seat and raised her arms to let the wind slam her, blast away the last of the home she was about to escape.

"I adore you!" Zee yelled.

He was twenty-one, but still looked to Amal like the boys at her high school: skinny, his hair untamed, his smile as if he had not yet contended with the world. Though he was as old as Amal's youngest brother, Adnan, who could run their father's tax prep agency the next day if he had to, about the only thing Zee knew how to run was his beloved car, a recent birthday gift from his parents.

She leaned over, kissed his cheek, and slipped on the embroidered tunic. As they exited the highway, she buttoned the top up to the neck. When they pulled up to the storefront mosque between Lovely's Paan & Chai Cafeteria and a grocery plastered with multilingual ads for lottery tickets and prepaid cell phones, she gathered her wind-tangled hair into a bun and wrapped the outfit's gauzy dupatta around her head.

The mosque's grilled glass door opened onto a bare-walled car-peted hall for communal prayers. Subduing their voices, Amal and Zee approached a low-lit hallway in the back. In a storeroom-slash-office, their two witnesses—Zee's chemistry lab partner and the goalie of his suburban soccer team—stood in fidgety deference by the imam's lac-quered walnut desk.

When the imam asked Zee if he accepted, Zee inquired if he should say "I accept" three times.

The imam recapped his pen and looked up from the paperwork. "If you wish."

The lab partner mumbled, "I think that's only in the movies, man."

The imam muttered that his takeout biryani was getting cold.

Still, Zee looked deep into Amal's eyes and said, "I accept," then said it again, and then again. Amal said she accepted without waiting for the imam to ask. Zee squeezed her hand and leaned in to kiss her, but the goalie cleared his throat and reminded him in decorous whisper, "mosque."

The imam dispensed with their business in blue ball point.

Amal and the guys rushed out of the mosque and into Lovely's. They snatched up the last four rosy gulab jamuns glistening in syrup in an alu-minum tray. They fed them to each other in celebration. Licking their fin-gers, they left the goalie's Kia in the strip lot and piled into Zee's car. They flew back to town up I-59 blasting Bollywood with the bass up and the top down.

Parked outside her parents' townhome, Amal composed herself. She took in the windows choked with heavy drapes by her privacy-obsessed mother, the concrete driveway that had been paved over a flowerbed by her father and car-obsessed older brothers, the mold-stained stucco that her parents balked at paying some guy a hundred and twenty plus tip to bleach clean, the security camera that had never caught a package thief but had been useful once in accusing her of breaking curfew. She hadn't cleared her room earlier that day so as not to raise any alarms. She told the guys to wait while she fetched her bags.

As she opened the car door, Zee placed his hand on her shoulder, his demeanor newly protective. Amal flinched. She hadn't planned on being his thing to take care of. When she stepped out of the car, Zee jumped out too, ready to lead the way into her childhood home. Why did men think that signing a paper suddenly shifted reality? Though, given how her mother caved to all her father's travesties, perhaps some women did too.

Zee had, so far, been unadulterated joy, time with him weightless.

They'd met two years ago on the beach in Galveston. Adnan had gathered his college friends and brought Amal along as a foil so he could hang out with his long-time girlfriend, Mariam. Mariam's parents were acquaintances of their parents, stalwart fellow Pakistanis, religiously observant. Mariam had brought her own friends down too, so as not to raise her father's suspicions that she was off on a tryst with Adnan.

Amal had planned to lose Adnan and Mariam's crowd as soon as they'd gathered—all local kids who'd never left the Houston area and, Amal imagined, would remain forever cemented there, inhaling highway exhaust and refinery fumes. She'd brought her running shoes, had planned to take off across the sands, headphones on, house music throbbing, salt air in her hair.

She did. And found Zee trailing her, then catching up. Perhaps Adnan had sent him to keep an eye on her. She pulled out her headphones. "I don't need watching."

"I know." He matched his pace to hers. "I'm Zeeshan."

"I know." She'd seen him around Adnan before. Thought about him afterwards, his easy untethered air. He threw out schemes as if he were free to be where he wanted, when he wanted, how he wanted, with whom he wanted. She'd wondered if nineteen was too old for sixteen.

"There's an ice cream place on the pier," he said, a bit out of breath.

She'd kept her pace, run on past the crowded pier toward a long out-cropping of rocks, up to the last boulder. She sat, barnacles scraping her calves, inhaling the must of seaweed, imagining herself at the very end of the world. Zee dropped down beside her. If he spoke now, broke her reverie, she would get up and run again, faster than he could keep up from what she'd gauged on the last stretch. He remained silent.

Since then, they'd never looked beyond the moment. She reveled in his impulsiveness. So far, it had been amusing, and since the events in her home over the last month, it had proven useful. Zee was an only son of a flamboyant Punjabi family—too liberal, in her parents' opinion—with deep pockets here and deeper roots back in Lahore. Zee knew his parents could afford to, and would indulge his every need, every mistake. His mother knew who to call. Consultants on hand for college admissions, lawyers on quick-dial for speeding tickets.

After their marriage ceremony, when Zee jumped out of the car ahead of her, Amal asked what he was doing.

"Carrying your bags down?" he proposed, surprise in his tone that she hadn't expected it. "I'll fight anyone who tries to stop us. Take you home!"

His friends whooped. She would have laughed if she knew that wouldn't hurt his pride. To him, this moment seemed to be, in all ear-nestness, a princess-rescue montage from a film.

Amal had never been anyone's princess. Not even her parents'. On report-card days, she was a merit badge on their self-worth but on most days, given her ways, a symbol of their shame. She showed too much leg, sometimes she showed belly; she'd been found smoking with unfath-omable goth girls; she'd been caught partying with boys. Her perfect A's would fade from her parents' psyche and their universe could tremble for hours, even days or months depending on the severity of her rebel-lion. They had no such meter for her three brothers who could only bring them joy, tempered with the occasional heartache, soon soothed by a new accomplishment. Her parents' sole objective seemed to be to keep her transgressions from getting so severe that the fallout might last them a lifetime. Her body was the vessel in which the family honor resided. Since she'd hit puberty, her mother bemoaned weekly her own failure to raise a modest girl, and her father had added to other potential punishments a vague threat to send her back to Pakistan, to her Dadi's house to be safely married off.

She'd done her father the favor herself on this day.

She hugged Zee. "I don't want you to fight anyone."

"No?"

"No."

"But will you be safe in there?"

She twirled her keys. "I've lived in that house for eighteen years, and I'm standing here, right?"

"If there's any sign of trouble, Zee," the chem lab partner called from the car, "we'll break in if we have to."

Zee looked between his friends and Amal. "But how will we know?"

"I'll yell out my window," she promised, bestowing on him a parting kiss, indulging his fantasy of a knight on duty beneath a turret. He nodded once, hands on hips, and scanned all egresses of the house.

Inside, Amal slammed the door and sallied through rooms with her customary ruckus. As she'd expected, no one looked up. If she'd been quieter, someone might have wondered who'd come in.

In the kitchen, her mother banged a cooking spoon against the rim of a pot, immersed in the preparation of her weekly Friday feast. She was expecting her sons to gather that evening. She'd given up asking Amal to help cook. She'd agreed to learn, but her mother had been short-tempered about how Amal's daal was too runny for her father, her parathas not crispy enough for this brother, her okra too slimy for that brother.

Amal heard a splash and sizzle of water in her mother's saucepan—she was amidst a delicate operation of gravy constitution, one that would require her sustained attention for several minutes. Which was all the time Amal needed. She hadn't packed, but she'd arranged everything so she could sweep it up into waiting bags. It was like an exhalation of a breath held too long, this leaving of the room that had felt for the last few years as if it were only on loan to her until she became someone else's responsibility. She had no idea what kind of accommodations she would be in with Zee, but she welcomed the unlatching of her present cage.

Dadi might be the only one who'd want to talk to her. She'd been walking in on Amal unannounced, and if Amal happened to look up as she was approaching, she would steady herself on doorframes and hall-way tables as if she had trouble making it across the length of the house, as if her girth of age was a newly destabilizing force on her joints. She'd lower herself creakily onto Amal's bed, some new justification on hand for why Amal shouldn't judge her father's recent behavior too harshly. She'd speak of these things in the Punjabi of their ancestral village as if she were digging into a more deeply rooted truth than city-people-Urdu could handle. Luckily, Dadi was on her prayer rug right then. Nothing could distract her except for a live fire.

The Animal Planet channel chattered away in the living room. Her father could watch nature documentaries forever. Especially ones that involved procreation. There was something on about penguins, so Amal knew he would be riveted. Penguins mated for life.

She scanned her closet one last time. Who knew when, if ever, she'd be allowed back into this house? She could hear her grandmother chant-ing through the closing verses of her prayer during which she got louder as if letting Allah know she was wrapping up her conversation for now and reentering the practical world until the next prayer time.

Amal wiped her vanity shelf free of makeup dust and concealer drips.

There, in front of the mirror, she laid down a copy of her nikahnama, the declaration of marriage from the mosque her only announcement of her planned desertion. Her father would not be able to argue on the grounds of propriety—with his second life and his second wife back in Pakistan. He'd kept his secret for a whole year. She'd only kept hers for an hour. What she'd just pulled, she told herself, was as halal, and as wrong as what he'd done.

Last month, the day before their grandmother's arrival in Houston, their father had admitted to their mother his second marriage back in Lahore. He had two ways of owning up: most often, he'd pull out his pocket comb, neaten his hair that he kept dyed a shiny black, and mumble that things had been the will of Allah; but occasionally, when he was too ashamed to mask his human failings, he would look away and bellow his confession in a tone of martyrdom-cum-bravado. He was in mode two that day.

Their father made his announcement to their mother behind closed doors. He'd needed to come clean because his new wife had been living with his mother in Lahore. Their mother let out such a wail that Adnan, who was home that afternoon, afraid that their father might have hit her, rushed to kick the door open. Their father had meted out beatings to his sons for their own good when they were young, and even Amal once when, at the age of fourteen, she'd returned at midnight in fishnets, mascara smudged, screaming, "Amy Winehouse is dead and nothing else matters!" Adnan had gripped his arm that night and told him to stop. But their father had never hit their mother before.

The master bedroom door smashed with Adnan's kick. Their mother ran out, tearing off her favorite apron on which she'd taught Amal to cross stitch a feeble peacock. Her long thinning braid flapping, she dashed blindly past Adnan and right into Amal.

Amal, some primal female instinct overtaking years of resentful distance from her mother, gathered the sunken-faced woman in her arms and steered her into her own room. Her mother, who'd grown up sisterless, collapsed in the shelter of her daughter's embrace. She fell on Amal's bed and cried fiery tears. She wouldn't say what it was as Amal stroked her head, her back.

Their father stomped up, opened his mouth in Amal's doorway, closed it again as dumbly as General, the goldfish he kept by the TV, then exited the house, slamming the front door behind him.

Adnan approached the threshold of Amal's room but would not enter that space full of his mother and sister, their fusing anguish, their pent-up condemnation. For many minutes, he made his large frame small by crossing his arms, hunching his shoulders, pacing outside with his head lowered. But finally, he beckoned Amal out.

"Turns out, he's married someone back home," he told her, agitated, embarrassed for their father. "It's been over a year." When Amal had no words, he tried, "Look, I know this sucks, but it's not like it's illegal back there."

Of course, Amal had heard the hushed anecdotes about men with four wives back in Pakistan, but she'd always had the impression that the practice was not taken lightly, nor looked on kindly by many. In the end though, it was tolerated—licensed by mullahs, blessed by mothers. Over the last few years, their father's annual trips back home had become biannual. To settle land claims, he'd said. Their mother used to accompany him every year, but for the last two years he'd stopped taking her. She'd begun making excuses to her mother about why she couldn't visit, something about needing to be home because this son and then that one had decisive exams coming up. But she'd never asked their father why. Amal wondered in that moment if their mother had always suspected the truth.

She found herself shaking from Adnan's words. She felt cold. Cold from the shock of mothering her mother; from her father's nonchalant upbraiding of her while he had carried on; from the revelation of which side of the line Adnan was on.

"Is that what you'll tell Mariam some day?" she asked.

"It's not like that." Adnan's face flushed. "He's from a different generation, you know?" Saying this, Adnan escaped, not back to his room, but throwing on the faded sweatshirt their mother hated, he left the house, hood up. It was as if he, too, must reluctantly bear the male burden of God-given rights.

Amal had known her mother would forgive her father. She was a wife first. That day, she had also become first-wife. She would mourn this elevation. Then she would embrace it, claim the privileges the status gave her over the second wife. Yes, her mother would forgive her husband. But Amal knew she could not forgive her father.

That afternoon, Amal's older brothers came over in anticipation of their grandmother's arrival the next day. It was the first night that their mother did not cook them a meal while they were in the house. She remained in her bedroom, a futile suitcase propping the broken door shut. Likely, the suitcase had been placed by her as a vague poetic threat, because that was the bag she travelled with to Pakistan. The boys ordered pizza.

Amal had no appetite. She clambered onto the roof outside her bedroom and texted Zee after a year of silence between them. *I miss you*, she told him the truth, crossing her fingers that he would text back.

She hadn't expected him to respond. Her mother had caught her last year in Zee's car, his hands under her shirt. Her mother dared not tell their father, but she yelled at Adnan that she would kill herself if her own son allowed his sister to be dishonored by his friend. Adnan had told Amal to cool it. He couldn't threaten her with much because he also knew that, though he might be okay if his relationship with Mariam was found out, Mariam would not be.

But after their mother's ultimatum, whatever Adnan had said to Zee that day ended the boys' friendship. Zee texted Amal his first and last *I love you*. She did not respond in kind, unable to say what she wasn't sure of yet. She sent him back jokey texts, which he acknowledged with a smiley face; then, over the next few days, pleading ones, which the maddening dots on her phone told her he began responses to but did not send; and then, over the following weeks, she sent serious ones, which he ignored altogether. She stopped.

After their father's confession, he had stayed out and didn't return until the next day, when he brought their grandmother home with him from the airport. The boys hugged her, and she told them she loved them very much. Amal kept her distance, picturing Dadi's days with her second daughter-in-law. Sometimes, when she couldn't stand this house bursting with her father's ego and her brothers' bluster, she'd wondered about a life in Pakistan, in the villa that her grandmother used to complain was too chilly and empty, lamented over long-distance phone calls how she wandered from room to room fluffing pillows on unused beds and replacing the decor seasonally to give the place a pretense of lives in motion. Amal's imagination had luxuriated at the thought of that much space and silence to herself. Now, with the occupation by the new wife, that fantasy, too, was closed to Amal.

In Houston, Dadi settled into one of the older boys' unused rooms, but she was not the only guest around the house. The spirit of the second wife had come with her; hung around the old woman like a sulking shadow, an uninvited plus-one.

On her second night, Dadi had come to her room, prayer rug in hand, and sat down on the bed while Amal was at her desk studying for her AP Economics test. "He's brought a little light into my last days," she said. "I was so alone."

Amal did not respond.

"He's my only son, and all he's done is his duty towards his aging mother," she added. Then she launched into her nighttime prayers right in Amal's room. In the break between her prayer rakats, she told Amal, "Don't worry, she's not as young as you, though I am hopeful for good news, given her health." After her prayers were over and Amal had still said nothing, not even turned around, her grandmother rolled up the prayer rug and said curtly, "You don't know things, so don't blame him so hard. Men have needs."

Amal tapped her foot fast to keep herself from bolting up from her desk and startling her grandmother as she was tempted to do. Women have needs too, she wanted to yell. But she couldn't bring herself to scandalize that rationalizing old heart. Talking back to her wouldn't be mere defiance like it was with her parents; coming from two generations down, it would be disrespect the equivalent of a slap. She decided her silence was a sufficiently rude rebuke.

To her surprise, Dadi didn't leave. Amal shut her laptop and spun her chair around. Perhaps the woman would see that she was disturbing her study. But noticing that she had Amal's attention, her grandmother eased out of her bosom a little key on a chain. She wheeled out a suitcase of hers that had been stashed in Amal's closet and unlocked it. After rooting around for a while among shopping bags from tasteful shops in Lahore, filled with gifts not in fact from those shops, she produced a neat crinkling cellophane package. Folded with precision inside was a henna-green embroidered silk outfit. She handed it to Amal with satisfaction.

Amal took it, thanked her, and set it aside on her desk.

"Open it, girl," her grandmother said, sitting down again. "She spent days helping me find the perfect design for you. The dyeing, the embroidery, the tailoring—she's the one who ran all over town for your sake."

There was only one "she" Dadi could have been referring to. Amal did not want to ask her name, lest her grandmother also suggest some form of respectful address for one's father's second wife.

"Why would she send me something?" Amal snapped.

"You'll be living with her soon, so she wanted to send you her welcome, her blessings. What else?"

Perhaps she'd misunderstood who Dadi had been referring to. "Who will I be living with?"

"Uff, me and your other mother, of course," her grandmother said. "Were you thinking of surprising me with your arrival?" She laughed. "Your father's been talking about it for a year now, telling me how much you're looking forward to moving after your high school graduation. He thinks she might be a good influence on you, and I agree—such a pious young woman."

Amal did not let her roiling insides reflect on her face. Misery finds its company and her grandmother had hers now. Amal hoped her father would return so infrequently that Dadi and the second wife would haunt the corridors of the villa in lockstep, awaiting him, aging together in their anticipation until they could not be told apart. She trained her attention back on her work and did not gratify her grandmother by opening the packet.

When the woman finally raised herself with a sigh and plodded out of the room, Amal flung aside her textbook, fell on her bed and tried Zee again. *I really need you.*

At midnight, her phone buzzed with a text. *Is this a mirage?*

She imagined those words in his voice as if he stood by her, like on the first windblown day when he'd said, "I know." Her body lit up as if his touch had returned. Zee was pure. Zee was pleasure. If he showed up on her street right then, she would run out and throw herself into his uncomplicated arms, not give a thought to who tore open which curtains to glower down. But she reined in her mad impetus. She needed to draw him back in gently, unwind her family's jinx on their relationship. This was not about a moment, but her life. If Zee was still Zee, he would be game for anything. She'd have to strategize for the both of them.

Barely a month later, with a final glance at her nikahnama, Amal picked up her gym bag bulging with shoes, a jumbo duffel bag bursting with clothes, and a tote bag of self-care items. Technically, Zee had more say in what happened to her from here on out than her father did. Within the community, she had gone from being expected to obey her father to being expected to obey her husband. Her father would know this well, but obedience and duty were not ideas Zee concerned himself with—if any. She felt featherlight at the thought of days and nights with him.

By the front door, the gym bag swiped the top of the shoe rack and knocked over her brothers' row of indoor flip-flops.

"Leaving?" Her father called from the living room, his face still to the TV.

Dadi started from her room at the sound of the toppling shoes. She clucked. "Children have so many bags here. Always doing things. Always busy. Can you carry all that yourself, girl?" She turned to the TV room. "Help your daughter, Saqlain."

Amal slammed the front door behind her, just as her father had.

Zee was waiting with the trunk open. "What did they say?" he asked, anxious at seeing her emerge in a rush.

She flung everything into the trunk and hopped into the front seat. "Go! Let's go!" She forced herself not to look back.

Zee laughed. "Who's up for wedding day margaritas?" he asked, forgetting his first question already.

Amal's phone buzzed with calls from her father, then texted threats to track her and show up at her location. She powered the phone off. Then at the I-59 onramp, she tossed it to the roadside scrub. Zee took her hand. "I'll get you a new one."

A new what, she thought to herself. She laced her fingers between his.

They drove to their favorite Tex-Mex place and stayed there until the sun went down and string lights crisscrossed the whole patio.

ZEE COULDN'T AFFORD a place of his own yet, but his parents let him move into their suburban home's pool house with his wife. They had helicopter-parented him his whole life, and so had a fine sense by now for how to balance his imagined need for independence with a safety net. They knew he was destined for greatness, if only they could get him through each year of schooling and they were tantalizingly close—he was only two semesters away from a dual business and chemistry degree with honors. This was hardly the time to yank the rug from under him and rip the roof from his head. His mother had the pool house carpeted and furnished in two days, and Amal and Zee moved out of his childhood bedroom into their own little place.

On the first night Zee had brought her home, Amal followed him through the vaulted foyer lit up by a stupendous chandelier. The house was stone quiet, as if in defiance of the lights. Amal worried about tracking dirt onto the pristine dark wood floors but there appeared to be nowhere to place outside shoes. Zee rambled in, saying his father was probably out as usual at a client dinner. He rapped on the door of his mother's study and introduced Amal.

Zeba came to the doorway. She wrapped a light shawl over her tank top, but did not step out. She was probably as old as Amal's mother but looked fifteen years younger. Amal decided that the three additional children her mother had borne in that decade and a half had drained her life force. Zeba's glow could be said to be manufactured: salon-highlighted waves, a discreet manicure, toned arms that looked courtesy of a personal trainer. But the incandescence in her eyes was her own, her soul still untired. She squinted at Amal. "I think I've met you before."

"Ji," Amal acknowledged politely, though her gut knotted up in mortification. On Zee's pool deck last spring, she'd been sharing a lounger with him when his mother and a friend had stepped out in bathing suits, sweating glasses of rosé in hand. As Zee and Amal tried to untangle from each other and from their towels, Zeba waved them off as if to tell them not to bother. She took her friend's hand and turned back in. Amal didn't want to begin this new relationship with Zeba by revisiting that first encounter. She remained quiet, hoping Zeba's memory for specifics was as bad as her own mother's.

"So, Mama, she's my wife," Zee said.

His mother stepped out then and looked from one to the other, pausing finally on Amal's face, scrutinizing her features for what felt like minutes.

Amal thought perhaps Zee's mother needed more proof, so she nudged him. "The other nikahnama?"

"Oh, I left it in the car." Zee sounded relieved as he whirled around.

Zeba shook her head at Amal. "I don't need your papers." Her hand on the doorknob, she added, "Tell him to come see me when he returns."

The second day, Zeba insisted on at least a private celebration of the marriage, ordered Zee's favorite takeout Mediterranean and texted his father, Nauman, to demand he dine at home that evening. He joined them in the formal dining room, bringing with him a surprise guest— Zeba's older brother, Abid.

Amal entered the dining room in a peach silk sari Zeba had lent her for the occasion and shown her how to pleat and tuck. She had guessed that Amal's simple mother had no experience in the art of donning a sari. She'd held diamond hoops up to Amal's earlobes, and then pulled them back, saying, "Too much." She gave her pearl drop earrings instead.

"These, you can keep. Your mother probably has many sets saved for you, but who knows if you'll ever give her the chance."

Amal's stomach turned. She set the earrings down on Zeba's vanity.

"Don't get me wrong," Zeba said, placing them back in Amal's palm and closing her fingers over them. "I have no plans to be your mother. Neither of us needs that." Amal looked up and noticed for the first time that Zeba wore a tiny nose stud just like her mother did. She'd always thought it so old fashioned on her mother. Maybe it was the austere gold of her simple round stud. Zeba's was a playful crescent moon of faceted silver.

In the dining room, Nauman appraised Amal's appearance and nodded at Zee. Abid Tarar, who had flown in from Lahore to visit his own son in New Haven, thumped his nephew on the shoulder and stated that his cousin could learn a thing or two from him. Zee appeared too stunned by the sight of Amal in his mother's sari to exchange manly laughter with his uncle. Nauman thumped his brother-in-law back, to make up for Zee's reserve; asked what the worry was—the boy was a Tarar after all. Zeba rubbed her temple and looked away.

Over dinner, Zeba, after a brief inquiry after Abid's wife, Iram, ignored the men for the rest of the meal and watched Amal instead. When Abid teased Nauman with his old college nickname of "No-man," Zeba did not bother to defend her husband. The men had been best friends, had had each other before this bond through Zeba.

As Zee and Amal did the dishes later, the three elders conferred in quiet tones over jasmine tea in the drawing room. Then they pulled Zee aside and told him that they drew the line at children. Those he was not allowed yet.

This was just fine with Amal. She couldn't picture a living being dependent on her for care. Even her father did not entrust General's feeding schedule to her and recruited Adnan when needed. She wondered if General was alright, given the probable state of the household after her actions, and then decided he was fine. Her father had always spoken more lovingly to the fish, named after several Pakistani presidents, than he had to her. So far, she preferred the shelter of Zee to her father's shadow. She'd married Zee for how they laughed together over everything and nothing, and for how he looked at her, really looked at her, when he made love to her.

Since their marriage though, there were times he was so ardent in bed, it was as if he were becoming the space around her. Sometimes he cried afterwards. This she would not miss if they were ever to part. His fervor dissipated into their tiny room, fogging it up like a kettle left on boil too long. Those nights she had a presentiment that she'd escaped from one borrowed space to another. She would walk out onto the balcony, iced tea in hand, the top sheet tied around her, leaving him to clean up and gather himself. Afterwards, he'd fall into such a deep sleep that he often missed class the next day.

On the balcony, Amal didn't worry that her in-laws might see her from the main house—they preferred the capacious interior of their home to their patios and their golf-course of a garden. Her own parents, too, had a deep appreciation for the luxury of climate-controlled interiors—wrangling the expanses of nature was not an entertainment, nor a noble pursuit where they came from. No one in her family understood her proclivity for camping and hiking, releasing her into the outdoors with her white classmates' families when she wore them out with her insistence. They accounted for her love of the wilderness to being born on American soil, the only one of their children.

At Zee's house, Amal wandered often to the creek at the edge of their property. She sent Adnan pictures of bedraggled water rats and skittish deer in the woods beyond. A week after she'd left home, Adnan had texted Zee to check if she was okay. Because that was all he'd asked, and not demanded to get in touch with her, Amal contacted him from her new phone and made him promise to keep it to himself.

Not that it mattered, Adnan told her, because their father had sworn not to speak with her and forbidden the household to mention her. *It'll blow over*, he assured her over text. *Doesn't it always?*

She hated the presumption in that last line. As if she'd simply stayed out late again and not chosen a whole new life. She didn't text him back and didn't talk to him for days afterwards. Meanwhile, to prove it all, though she wouldn't be able to say prove exactly what, because she didn't quite think of herself as a wife in the manner of her mother, she tidied their room while Zee was at school and even picked up his laundry and brought it into the main house.

"Are those Zeeshan's clothes?" Zeba asked, pausing on her way to her morning swim. "Just drop them in the hamper in the laundry room. That's what he does."

"You don't have to do it," Amal protested. It's the little things, she thought. She'd have to get Zeba used to a new order, break one habit at a time.

"Why would I?" Zeba said. "The housekeeper will be in tomorrow. You can leave yours here too."

So, that's how Zee's clothes ended back up in their closet, neatly stacked. Amal acknowledged some relief that it wasn't Zeba who brought his clothes in when they were out, and a sheepish joy that she needn't bother with his laundry after all, keep up with the folding regimen he was used to, underwear included.

The next weekend Adnan took Zee out for collegial drinks, treated him like a friend again. She knew then that her brother had understood, knew the place he should give her decision, the space she needed. He did text her finally, to tell her that General had died.

She was tempted to ask how it could've happened, given their father's diligence. Instead, she looked up the lifespan of a goldfish, then consoled Adnan with the observation that a goldfish kept in a bowl will only live so long. To cheer him up, she sent him a picture of a muddy armadillo.

She'd startled the critter as she was poking the waters behind the house with a fallen branch. It dunked underwater and scooted away, so she waded in and followed it across into a thicket of weeds and young longleaf pines. Zeba had appeared at the creek that day, informing her that the owners of the undeveloped property on that side were not shy with their guns. Amal was disappointed at the idea of civilization on the other side of a mysterious creek she had dared to cross on her own, at the knowledge that the woods were owned by somebody, and perhaps most so that her crossing had not gone undetected by her mother-in-law.

One night, as Amal leaned on the balcony railing, she noticed steam dissipating out of a window of the kitchen of the main house. It was past midnight. She exchanged her sheet for pajamas and tucked the comforter around Zee who had fallen into one of his death sleeps. From the deck outside the kitchen, Amal rose on tiptoe and peered into the arched glass cutout of the backdoor just as Zeba dropped an entire chicken into a stock pot. The counter was resplendent with onion skins and ginger peels and powdery spills from spice bottles. Amal knocked.

On porch rockers outside the kitchen, jewel-cut scotch tumblers in hand, Zeba described for Amal how to make broth for yakhni pulao. She said that to extract the essence of the bones fully, it was important to do this at the time you most felt like it—the yakhni needed to know you meant it; intention was everything.

Zeba twirled her tumbler so it caught the warm light that spilled out of the kitchen and threw it over them in a dance of diamonds. She was watching Amal, who was getting used to this by now. But that night, Amal noticed an agitation in Zeba's eyes. Her mind raced trying to fathom Zeba's thoughts. She was transfixed, found herself aching to learn anything Zeba might be willing to teach her. But she was also afraid; Zeba was measuring her worthiness.

Zeba set her empty glass down, leaned forward and asked, "What is it going to take for you to give me my son back?" She told Amal that her son was her life's work, the only reason she'd endured her husband all these years. "You're a distraction to him."

For one relief-flooded minute Amal pictured herself entirely unbound, on the road to who-knows-where. But she couldn't deny the most practical reason she'd needed Zee. For a place to rest. For a home base from which she might wander at will. She admitted to Zeba that Zee had missed some school. "I could help him focus again," she said. "He'd do anything for me. He loves me."

"But you don't love him," Zeba said quietly. She searched Amal's face. "Those eyes of yours—always on the horizon."

Amal thought she should resent Zeba's words. But, somehow, she felt seen rather than seen through. As if Zeba recognized her deepest inclinations. Still, this was the choice she had made. "I'm happy with him."

"And without him? What would you do without him?"

Unable to hold her gaze, Amal looked instead at Zeba's crescent moon stud twinkling in the night light.

Zeba leaned in close again, took Amal's chin and tapped gently on her left nostril. "A nose built for a jewel. Would you like to get it pierced?"

Amal drew in a sharp breath at her touch, and her proposal. Her mother had had her ears pierced as a newborn. She'd been waiting to turn eighteen to get cartilage piercings, a wing tattooed by her ankle, but she'd never considered this. She nodded. "I guess I know some places. Up on Westheimer?"

Zeba swatted at the idea as if it were a fly. "My friend Sarah? You saw her that one day at the pool." She laughed, likely recalling the incident Amal had been desperate for her to forget. "She'll do it. I trust only her hands."

FOR THE NEXT TWO WEEKS, Amal pulled out her AP books again. She couldn't hear Zee when he spoke to her. She felt as if she'd fallen back to earth from a honeymoon they'd never taken. She stared at her textbooks as if they were new to her. She flipped to parts that were too hard to grasp and recited them in a trance. She laid them end-to-end with her notebooks and binders on the pool house balcony and walked back and forth across them as if they were a balance beam. That night on the kitchen porch, she'd worried that Zeba's words—about being without Zee—would ring in her head. She found herself haunted instead by *intention is everything*, tried at all hours to make meaning of it and lost its meaning by repeating it in an endless loop as she walked on her book beam. *intention is everything is intention is everything is intention…*

"Hey!" Zeba was waving at her from the kitchen porch.

Barefoot, Amal ran across the lawn to the main house. She'd seen Sarah's Range Rover pull into the driveway.

Sarah had come with her kit. Zeba set up a station at the kitchen counter and directed Amal to a barstool. She opened a small velvet box. A miniature seed of a gold nose stud winked up at Amal.

Sarah pumped the foot lever of the barstool to lower Amal to a satisfactory height.

As Sarah steadied her left hand on the bridge of Amal's nose, Zeba placed her hand on Amal's. "Scared?"

Amal shook her head.

Sarah pulled her hand away. "Do. Not. Move. Do. Not. Speak." She began again.

As the point of the Sarah's needle came to rest on Amal's nostril, Zeba said, "Have you thought about what I asked you?"

Amal blinked. Sarah's needle pierced through. Amal's eye's teared up, her nose flushed hot. Sarah handed her a tissue and slid in the stud.

Amal did not dab at her eyes. She stared at Zeba. "About leaving Zee?"

"About what you would do without him." Zeba inspected the bejeweled puncture and then handed her a compact mirror.

"It's a good question you know," Sarah said, repacking her kit. "The way he drives that car."

Amal stood and looked from Sarah to Zeba and back again. "How can you imagine a horrid thing like that?"

"Oh, I imagine it all the time," Zeba said, dropping to the bar stool. "I'm his mother. I have no bigger fear."

Sarah set down her tools and rubbed Zeba's shoulders in gentle circles. Then she kissed the top of Zeba's head and walked off to pour two glasses of chardonnay.

What shook Amal, flooded her with guilt, was that she had pondered that very scenario as she was walking her beam that morning. The open road she had imagined when Zeba had asked her to leave Zee the other night led into nothingness. Not a field of possibilities, but an engulfing darkness. When she tried to picture it, she was not able to see herself, not in this place, nor headed anywhere else.

Sarah handed a glass to Zeba and took her own wine to the TV lounge.

Zeba took a sip. "You'll break his heart one day. Do it now."

"But he's happy with me," Amal tried the argument she'd been making to herself.

"Leave him to me." Zeba set her glass down. "I've helped him get over lost toys before."

Amal knew by now that though Zeba was wife half-heartedly, she was mother whole-heartedly. Zeba needed Zee more than she did. Amal was about to treat Zee abominably and she was already sorry. She would allow herself to be sorry now so she could be less burdened with guilt later, when Zee might become the failure Zeba feared.

Amal returned Zeba's gaze and weighed her next question. She took a deep breath. "Will you send me to college?"

For a year, Zeba showed Amal the secrets of her kitchen and helped her with her college applications. Zee was confused about the divorce filing. The women broke it to him inside the big house, at a glorious tea party just for the three of them that Amal and Zeba prepared together. Samosas from scratch. Shami kababs. Kheer. He wanted to know if he'd failed them both by not graduating that year as he should have. His mother assured him that every day was a new day.

Two weeks after she turned nineteen, Amal carried her bags down the steps of Zee's pool house. Adnan helped her load them into his car and drove her to Austin.

The Renaming of Tooti Sadak

SIANAPUR BY LAHORE, 1989

The wooden warrior had fallen across the road.

Ma and Bhen, the town guards, stood over the warrior in the respectful silence of ironed khakis and polished boots and precisely angled berets. They stood in the devastated silence of those who have hoped. In the yet unsullied dawn, the warrior lay irreparably broken, joints crumbled to dust. Dust cannot be reassembled.

With the butt of his rifle, Bhen nudged one of the arms. It dislodged from the shoulder and rolled away at an angle, stopping as its extended fingers pointed toward the train station.

"Bhatka Khan," croaked Ma, glancing at the station. "We should send for him." He felt heavy with shame, not a personal regret, but as if it were soaking into him with the morning fog lurking in the streets.

"Of course." Bhen's whisper was a dispirited whistle. "But, where's Chhota?"

As if he had heard, Chhota emerged from the station in freshly-scrubbed eleven-year-old glory. Even at that distance, MaBhen, as the pair of guards were known, could see that Chhota had tidied himself for the town celebration. The boy's shirt was buttoned up to its frayed collar and tucked into trousers that were not rolled up as usual. His wiry hair had been oiled and combed down flat.

Chhota did not get close enough to MaBhen to receive any instructions or explanations. Halfway between the station and the road, he saw for himself what had befallen the people of the town. He took in the sight of the warrior's beckoning arm and dashed back to the station.

He did not know what he would tell Bhatka Khan when he got back to their room. But then again, he and Bhatka Khan rarely had use for words.

EVEN THE DAY BHATKA KHAN had first appeared had been one of few words between them.

Chhota was racing down the platform of the train station, a pilfered roti crumpled in his hand. Moeen, the rotten-toothed snack stall owner, skittered after him. As Chhota streaked past a black-turbaned stranger who sat leaning against the station wall, he was distracted. He stumbled, fell face down, and flipped to see Moeen looming.

He would not return the roti to Moeen. This was not because of the hunger that had become one with his body over the last seven years, but because Moeen had teased him yet again about how his mother had abandoned him at the station and taken the same train right back to Lahore. When Chhota retorted that Mirza-the-mechanic had always told him his mother would return for him, Moeen snorted, "What is he, your father?" Then he laughed. "The mechanic lost his mind when he lost his girl. He sits drumming the trunk of that jujube tree all day eating berries that are so ripe and so rotten by the sun that they make his head spin. Then he makes up foolish stories for foolish children like you." At that, Chhota had grabbed a roti from the basket at the stall and run. He knew this would needle Moeen more than any words he could hurl back.

Meeting Moeen's eye as the man raised his fist, Chhota cracked his mouth wide open, even though the blood trickled again from the corner of his lip from the last cut Moeen had given him. He stuffed the entire roti into his mouth. Then he scrunched his eyes closed. A shuffle, and then a distant thud. Chhota opened his eyes. The turbaned stranger, and not Moeen, stood over him. The man's eyes were on the tracks, so Chhota propped himself up to look.

Moeen lay sprawled on the tracks moaning, his foot twisted at an odd angle. The smoke of an approaching train broke the horizon. Moeen shuffled toward the edge of the tracks on his behind. Too far below the platform to pull himself up, he raised his arms toward the stranger, the way a child asks to be picked up by its mother. The stranger, unmoved, returned to where he had been resting and leaned against the wall again.

The train whistled forward, ignorant, merry. Moeen waved his arms at the world in general now. So, it fell upon Chhota to rescue Moeen. He clasped the man's hands and pulled him with his entire weight. Back on the platform, Moeen, too ashen to challenge the stranger, hobbled back to his snack shop.

He did pause to squint at Chhota. "We're even, Asad," he said. "You owe me nothing as of this moment."

Chhota was tempted to quip that he would have liked a few more rotis in exchange for saving the man's life. But Moeen had addressed him by the name inked on a scrap of paper folded in the tarnished silver locket that had hung from the boy's neck for as long as he could remember.

As the train screeched into the station, the stranger asked Chhota, "Is there someone who would offer a roof to a passing visitor?"

That was the only day Chhota did not make himself available to the passengers, even though he depended on their handouts. Instead, he led the man to the storage room that served as his shelter—over the years it had become known as Chhota's room. Occasionally, storage space was needed for bundles of supplies for the snack shop or the operation of the station. These would be dumped in Chhota's room without his permission. Chhota was tolerated in that hutch in the manner of a stray cat adopted by the station.

Chhota led the visitor to his room, who, upon entering, set his satchel down under its barred window. Chhota perched on a concrete ledge that was his bed, watching. The man took out a carved metal frame and placed it in a nook in the wall. He swung open miniature doors on the frame, revealing a mirror. From a fold in his turban, he eased out a train ticket and tucked it in a corner of the mirror. Then he lugged some supply boxes together under the window, unwound his turban, and lay down the fabric to mark his resting place.

SUBSISTING ON SCRAPS from the station that Chhota shared with him, the stranger silently wandered the narrow dirt streets in his first days there. The townspeople probed Moeen for information, but he refused to address the matter, bitter about the supplies he could not reclaim because he dare not disturb the stranger's place of rest, but also enjoying the air of collusion and mystery that tied him to the man's presence, occasionally venturing to imply that he had permitted Chhota to host him.

The townspeople tried asking Chhota when the man planned to catch a train again. Chhota shrugged and did not admit to the number of times he had snuck the ticket from the mirror and tried to ascertain its validity. Unable to read, he would run his finger over the lettering as if this act might lead to a revelation. With the visitor's arrival, the rhythms of Chhota's survival had morphed into a game of treasure hunting. He had twice the amount of food to scrounge from the trains, relishing playing host. He remained even more vigilant for abandoned objects. The stranger could often utilize these finds for their room, or else he tersely proposed a wicked use, often involving Moeen, that made Chhota laugh. The street boys stopped calling Chhota an unwanted bastard and began treating him with the deference afforded to an assistant to a visiting official.

The peoples' curiosity about the stranger superseded even their daily obsession over a recent provincial election. The infighting about the election had frequently devolved from old men's derisive words to young men's fists to children's rocks. But, since the stranger, they put aside their differences in mutual hope of clues from the station. One day, tired of being questioned about the stranger's identity, Moeen demanded what use a bhatka hua, a lost wanderer, had for a name.

BHATKA KHAN ACQUIRED HIS NAME on the same day as Tooti Sadak did—the morning he ventured out before sunrise to see a barbed wire fence cutting across the main road that ran through the town. This road, that separated the river side of town from the train side, was referred to simply as Bari Sadak, the big road.

The townspeople awoke to the news that Bari Sadak had been split. The barrier extended all the way from the highway, which flanked one side of town, to the woods, which flanked the other. The barbed wire made it impossible to cross from one side to the other without walking a mile to the highway or risking the nettle and snakes in the woods. The townspeople had known that this would come to be; yet, they were shaken by the material presence of the divide.

The news spread that the barrier had been installed overnight by Tarar Sahib, an ambitious provincial government minister who had recently won the local district seat. Before the election, Tarar Sahib had been only a name to them, and after the election he had, so far, maintained his benevolent absence.

Two men from the town, one from the river side and one from the train side, had run for this district seat as well. Funds were collected by these candidates, and soon the rivalry between the sides ran so rampant that the river side—keepers of the town's waters—began to fly a blue flag. In response, the train side—lords of brick and rust—flew their own red flag. But the whole town took collective pride in the river by which it had been founded, and the train station by which it thrived. These shared passions caused the red flag to be dotted with a blue circle, and the blue flag to be dotted with a red circle. Thus, it came to be that each side was, of a sudden, saddled with an identity.

Youth around the town began sporting headbands of their flags, sewn by their women by the light of kerosene lamps and the heat of indignation in their bosoms. Once the headbands were donned, it was only natural that daily fistfights would ensue, peppered with the occasional gunfight. And while the two local candidates stood by in awe of what they had wrought, Tarar Sahib, a well-connected young industrialist, had the seat confirmed in his name by lining the appropriate federal pockets. Then he had his two competitors arrested on charges of corruption, and only facilitated their acquittal once they had turned over all the election funds they had garnered from the townspeople.

After the election though, Tarar Sahib found the town and its warring sides too much of a distraction. Typical of the big-heartedness his family was famed for, he offered to reinvest all the election donations back into a solution for keeping the peace. A man who identified himself as Tarar Sahib's foreman arrived by train one day and announced that their donations had been determined to be just sufficient for a barbed wire barrier between the two sides. With much ceremony, he added that Tarar Sahib would even put up his own money for high quality, imported barbed wire because he believed that this town had suffered enough and only a brute would cheat them on the quality of the necessary barrier.

The morning the barrier appeared, townspeople from both sides gathered at the stump of a jujube tree that had stood for decades in the middle of Bari Sadak. The tree had served as a shady, berry-littered traffic circle for bicycles and donkey carts and had lately become the afternoon proselytizing and napping spot for the mechanic. The tree had been injured so grievously in the fighting during the elections that it had to be cut down, flinging crazy-Mirza into a bout of ascetic reclusion. But the stump of the tree was rooted too deeply according to the boys who had been tasked with the cutting, and so it was left anchored in place, no one having bothered to challenge the boys, who returned to their cricket game as soon as they were done hauling the debris to their mothers for firewood.

Tarar Sahib's foreman had overheard the townspeople from both sides fret in shame over the fate of the ancient tree. Not wanting to be accused of favoritism by leaving the stump on either side of the barrier, he recommended that the fence be stopped on one side of the stump and begun again on the other. Unfortunately, this left the stump as an open access point between the two sides. So, Tarar Sahib, in his wisdom, advised his foreman to find a guard, one from each side of town, to be installed at the stump from sunrise to sunset on the government's pay. Tarar Sahib had an announcement posted that nighttime guards would not be needed because, after sundown prayers, people had their own familial disagreements to attend to.

Thus it was that the morning of the barrier, the townspeople also found, guarding the stump, a man from each side. Each guard was newly attired in a similarly-sized khaki uniform, too baggy for one, and too snug for the other, with a smart beret that matched the election flag of his side.

When Mirza ventured out of his dwelling and approached the stump, the two guards stood at attention, somewhat unsure whether their mutual gesture was out of respect for the wise madman, or a concern that they should stop him from clambering over to the train side. They were spared the conundrum however, because all the mechanic did was wave a broomstick at the people on both sides and then stab the road with it. "Toot gayi," he said, "Badi Sadak toot gayi." Badi Sadak is broken, he continued his rant, trailing his broomstick behind him all the way back to his rooms. Others, too, eventually drifted away to their homes and shops, the road now etched in their minds as Tooti Sadak.

On the train side, only Chhota and his guest remained with the guards. The wanderer looked up and down the barrier, and then pulled out some paper and tobacco from his pocket and proceeded to roll himself a cigarette.

"Ay, Bhatka Khan," said the guard on the train side who had heard Moeen dismiss the stranger as a bhatka hua, "got another?"

Bhatka Khan did not object to his new name and, handing the guard the cigarette he had just rolled, began to roll another.

"Oy, Bhatka Khan," said the guard on the river-side, "the cement under the barrier hasn't firmed up yet and you're already taking sides."

Bhatka Khan clambered on the tree stump, gave him the second cigarette, and then squatted there making a third for himself. The three men smoked in silence. When Bhatka Khan was done, he signaled Chhota to fetch his satchel from their room. The two guards, having finished their cigarettes, began to argue over whether Bhatka Khan should be allowed on the stump. By the time Chhota returned, they had determined that since Bhatka Khan was neither from the river side, nor the train side, but rather from the outside, they were not obliged to remove him.

From his satchel, Bhatka Khan retrieved a knife and began to peel away at the bark of the tree stump. By sundown, he had carved a beret on its top. The beret had a dot in it. This set off an argument between the guards. As Bhatka Khan headed back to the station, they could be heard yelling.

"Ay, ma-chod," said the guard from the train side, calling the other a motherfucker. "He's carved a red cap with a blue dot."

"Oy, bhen-chod," said the guard from the river side, calling the first a sisterfucker. "It's a blue cap with a red dot."

Bhatka Khan never did clarify which it was as he continued to work on the stump day after day. The guards declared Bhatka Khan's sculpture a warrior and he did not counter them on this either. Mirza broke out of his sulking retreat and began checking on the progress of the warrior with as much concern as he used to check the tree for signs of new growth.

The guards settled into a comfortable daily routine by the emerging warrior and simplified their expletives to ma and bhen—it was too hot for longer words. Soon, that was how they came to refer to each other, no matter their mood. Over shared lunches, over card games and cigarettes with Bhatka Khan, one became Ma, and the other Bhen. Even the townspeople got accustomed to their repartee, and the guards acquired the collective moniker of MaBhen.

When someone needed updates on gossip from the river side or had to pass on an urgent message, they asked Chhota to get down to MaBhen and slipped him a piece of fruit for his trouble. Chhota would relay the news to MaBhen in the presence of the warrior and save the fruit for Bhatka Khan who preferred it to all other sustenance besides his cigarettes.

"Why do you do this for him, eh?" Moeen leered at Chhota every now and then. "What's in it for you, boy?"

Chhota ignored Moeen, but at night, when the starlight shone through the window and lit up a patch between him and Bhatka Khan, he sometimes spoke, hoping for a hint on his plans. "Kalim Bhai, your ticket grows old."

"Who says, Asad?" Bhatka Khan muttered back. The two only referred to each other by their given names in the room where they had first learned them, each name too big for the persons the world assumed them to be, each of them content to reveal his identity only to those who could regard it.

When Chhota had first shown him to the room, the stranger had terrified him by grabbing the locket at his neck. Chhota had almost bit the man's hand, not ready to part with the only object in the world he knew to be his own. But the man held his shoulder and asked him to calm down; he only wanted to see. Inside the locket the man found the paper.

"They named you lion." He clicked the locket close again. "They had hope for you."

"How do you know?" Chhota wriggled away.

The man kneeled in front of the boy then and untucked a book-shaped locket from under his own collar. He unlatched it to show Chhota a faded scrap of parchment. "See? My people named me Kalim. They destined me to speak."

"What do you speak?"

The stranger chuckled hoarsely, startling Chhota. "Now that I am grown, I simply speak what I see. Sometimes, that is the truth."

"And sometimes it is not?"

"That depends on the listener."

"What do you see about me?"

"That when you are grown, you will wear your name on the outside too."

Chhota quietly began to think of himself as Asad. And relished being the only one privy to the name Bhatka Khan's people had given him. He began to listen closely to what his new friend told other people, turning it into a guessing game about all it could mean. This was especially amusing when Bhatka Khan bantered with MaBhen.

TARAR SAHIB'S FOREMAN descended on the town a few weeks after the installation to inspect the barrier. He came by himself on the last train and marched to the stump. There, he saw MaBhen busy with a game of poker as Chhota watched. Bhatka Khan was crouched on the stump, carving the tip of the warrior's sword. (He had decided to humor MaBhen's vision of the warrior and reworked the gun he had started into a sword, which was more noble.)

The foreman would not have liked the look of Bhatka Khan no matter what. But when he saw him freely perched on the stump, he yanked out a ball-point from his trouser pocket to make urgent notes on a pad. Scribbling with theatrical flair, he threatened to have MaBhen arrested for lapsing in their duties.

The guards, having developed a sense of ownership over the barrier, saw that Chhota watched their next move with the eyes of the townspeople. Drawing bravado from the warrior, they told the foreman to tuck his limp instrument back in his pocket and send Tarar Sahib to inspect his works himself.

The foreman spat on the ground several times and floundered for his next move. He saw no option but to pull out the ultimate threat from Tarar Sahib's book. He grabbed Chhota by the arm and told the guards that they and their families could be dragged away for treason and shot.

He cocked his fingers in imitation of a pistol and pointed at Chhota's temple, making eyes at MaBhen as if Chhota were their little brother. He began to laugh as Chhota wriggled and squealed to be let go. Bhatka Khan descended from the warrior and, taking the foreman's head in the crook of his arm, felled him dead with a single twist to the neck. Then he returned to pick up the cigarette he had dropped.

Chhota, one eye on the body as if it might shudder back to life, gathered Bhatka Khan's tools into his satchel and squatted down close to him. MaBhen, shaken and unsure, stepped away from the barrier and put some distance between themselves and Bhatka Khan. They had begun to trust him.

"The night does strange things to one's head." Ma fidgeted with his beret.

"The cock's crow might come with better answers." Bhen's voice sank with the sun.

They left Bhatka Khan smoking next to the body, one comforting hand on Chhota's shoulder.

When the guards returned at dawn, the body still lay on the train side.

They had slept on their fears, and the emerging daylight had a dissipating effect on their nightmares. They wished Bhatka Khan was around to help them and considered calling him over. But they were afraid of causing a commotion in town. Tarar Sahib's foreman was probably expected back on the first train that morning. They had to act before the trains began to arrive.

Bhen shoved the body over the stump toward the river side. Its legs landed on the barbed wire as it flopped over. Ma hoisted it down, shredding the legs in the process. No matter. He dragged the body toward the river while Bhen kept a lookout, and then returned to rest against the warrior, out of breath. Bhatka Khan showed up at his usual time, tangerines in hand, one for himself and one for each of them. He didn't ask about the body, and they didn't say. The three men peeled the tangerines and refreshed themselves with the scent of the fruit's torn skin.

Later that week, Moeen visited the warrior to inform MaBhen that someone had come to inquire after the foreman. Chhota, who was watching Bhatka Khan put the finishing touches on the warrior, quipped that the foreman had probably been dragged away for treason and shot. MaBhen mumbled their agreement. Bhatka Khan jumped off the warrior and clapped once loudly, as if to signal completion and admiration in a single gesture. Then he put his arm around Moeen's shoulder with a firmness that silenced Moeen, and walked him back to the station.

The next day another messenger from Tarar Sahib arrived on the train that pulled in at high noon. While the train idled, he left a brisk message with Moeen that since the tax revenues from the town did not support MaBhen's salaries, Tarar Sahib had decided to take down the barrier before the week's end and leave the townspeople to their own mercy. Then the messenger hopped back on the train right before it pulled away.

Mirza consoled the townspeople, who had by now wrapped the barbed wire into their daily routines. In fact, he advised them, they should prepare for a celebration on the day of the removal, that it could be a new beginning. Moeen assured everyone that he would inform the town as soon as there was any sign of Tarar Sahib's men arriving to remove the barrier.

He failed to do so, because the very next night they came in trucks from the highway. They ripped out the barrier like a backbone from a fish. They paid no heed to a mutilated tree stump in their way.

People tossed in their beds at the rumbling and the tearing but dared not step out of their homes. They told themselves that though the barrier had cost them a lot of money, the mechanic was probably right. They remained in bed, looking forward to donning their clean Friday outfits and meeting to rejoice in the reopening of Tooti Sadak.

By the time Chhota arrived at the scene of the fallen warrior, people had begun to gather. The two guards were circling the disaster, their voices accusatory.

"How could it fall just like that, Ma?"

"Clearly, Bhen, some harami felled it on purpose."

Someone from the train side set off a cry. "The warrior has been felled!"

Other people ran out, half-dressed, distraught but hardly surprised. It was as if their grief had been soaked in by the warrior as he overheard the stories that were relayed via MaBhen. And then, all their accumulated sorrows had flown out of his cracked body overnight, flitting under their doorways, seeping under their quilts, weighing down their hearts once more.

From the river side, a boy cried out, "The train side must have felled the warrior because Bhatka Khan had made him in our image."

MaBhen stared at each other, dropping all pretense.

"Ay, bhen-chod," Ma uttered the full curse, "is this your doing?"

"Oy, ma-chod, what do you think?"

A clump of asphalt from the torn-up road was thrown, and then another. Chhota hid his face and ran back to the station.

Passing Chhota in the opposite direction, Bhatka Khan cut through the crowd. The rock fight paused. He kneeled by the warrior and inspected its base and the shattered joints.

Then he stood up, his face dark, and looked around—not at the people, but further out. He searched the horizon, first this way and then that, as if evaluating the best direction to take.

Turning to MaBhen, he informed them, "Hollowed out by worms on the inside. The roots could hold no longer."

Commotion ensued as Bhatka Khan took long strides back to Chhota's room. Moeen condemned MaBhen for not protecting the warrior as the barrier was being torn down. He waited for the others to join him. But MaBhen were by now feared by most because they knew every secret. With one exchanged glance, they agreed that they were the only officials around. They ordered Moeen back to the station to keep an eye out for troubling strangers and requested that the women proceed with the preparation of the celebratory sweets as planned. The ruffians who had been flinging ripped concrete at each other were put to work brushing the debris off the road. And Mirza watched with contentment as MaBehn took charge of the reopening of Tooti Sadak.

AT THE STATION, BHATKA KHAN found Chhota sitting cross-legged on the floor of their room, holding the mirror frame to his chest. He said nothing to the boy but proceeded to remove the fabric of his turban from his bed. He folded it into neat creases, placed one end on his forehead and began to wrap it around his head.

"What are you doing?" Chhota asked.

On the boxes that were naked again lay a dagger in its leather sheath, one that Chhota had found on a night train, one that Bhatka Khan had taken without a word and never explained the use of. Bhatka Khan placed the dagger by Chhota. "This will be of use, but not with Moeen. He saw your mother leave and gave you bread and milk until others would." Then he eased the mirror out of the boy's arms.

"Did you come to look for me?" Chhota asked,

Bhatka Khan retrieved the train ticket. "You are not lost, so you cannot be found."

"Don't go. MaBhen will cry for you."

"They have each other." Bhatka Khan headed for the door.

"Your ticket is old." Chhota knew that the ticket was useless by now because the letters on it had been rubbed away by his fingers.

"Who says?" Bhatka Khan tucked the ticket into a fold of his turban.

As the man ducked under the door frame, Chhota called out, "Kalim Bhai…"

Bhatka Khan turned to look at him.

After a long moment, Chhota said, "The conductor on the noon train is always asleep from the heat."

Bhatka Khan nodded and was gone.

CHHOTA HAD BEEN RIGHT. MaBhen did miss Bhatka Khan. Thus it was that under their orders, Tooti Sadak, which was not divided anymore, was renamed Bhatki Sadak.

A Legal Alien

Houston, 2018

When Immigration and Customs Enforcement descended on our nook of Houston, we knew one of us would be taken: we were all brown. That we had nothing to hide, that we had each placed everything we loved on the mortgage lender's table for our three-thousand-square-foot patch of America, did not matter in those days. That we voted in every election, that some of us had even voted in this eventuality, did not signify in that season of terror. The ICE-men flew through our streets in packs, as if they had been uncaged to fulfill their destiny.

At first, we put on our best American accents. We got neat haircuts. We extracted our US passport cards from dusty corners of our wives' jewelry safes and slid them into the ID windows of our wallets, relegating our Texas drivers' licenses to the credit card slots. We stopped speeding. We started weeding, our exemplary flowerbeds proving the model citizens we were. Still, one of us had to go. Chugging beer as Mo grilled sausages on his patio, we mulled over Yasir as our best bet.

This was the kind of determination it took to carry on in America, to carry on America. We'd burnt our bridges, chosen our home, but failed to see the bones it was built from, the congealed blood it was cemented with. *Kher, der aaye, durust aaye.* Now we knew.

A student fresh from Pakistan, Yasir was renting a garage apartment from Mohammed Ayub while he attended Rice. In fact, it was Mo himself who offered him up. The boy hadn't yet discovered the grey areas that made non-halal meat permissible. Nor had any of our daughters shown an interest in his acne-ridden profile, and Mo and Noreen's little Tina was too young. (Some of us had thought it wasn't quite appropriate that they'd let a college boy stay with them, what with a prepubescent daughter at home, but the Ayubs were more-modern-than-thou, and with them, one either kept up or shut up.) Someone inquired whether Yasir was intelligent, but Mo couldn't be sure. Out of considerations, we concluded that he was the least fit among us to be American.

Problem was, his passport had an F-1 student visa stamped into it with galling neatness. (Mo had dashed up the spiral staircase of his garage and brought the passport to pass around.) Boy hadn't been a single place—he had one exit stamp from Lahore International, a transit stamp from Dubai International and one entry stamp at Bush International. Then someone pointed out that determining his status wasn't our job; all we had to do was bring him to their attention.

The next time ICE cruised down our street, Mo sauntered out with his hedge clippers and nodded at their passing SUV. Sensing a summons, they pulled over and approached him, all jeans and Kevlar vests. Mo paused by his well-tamed confederate jasmine vine and dropped that he had a new international student staying with him. From Pakistan, he clarified, without being asked.

"Is he in?" they inquired.

"Not sure," Mo said. "He's so quiet—spends a lot of time on his laptop."

So, they requested to search his room. Mo, being the homeowner, gave them permission and didn't even bring up warrants, despite the warnings splashed all over Facebook by pro-bono immigration lawyers.

They walked away with the boy's laptop that day, and they walked away with the boy the next. They haven't returned to the neighborhood since.

Over thin salty lassi and tandoori chicken so spicy it drew sweat from our brows, we agreed that Yasir would be fine. He had a rich aunt, a US citizen by now, somewhere in Sugar Land. Her lawyer husband grinned down at us from billboards proclaiming, *With Nauman, You're Not No Man.* Besides, the boy was young enough to start his life anew—if they released him and sent him back to Pakistan.

Talking with Boys

We suspected nothing when my sister Sana was born. The baby seemed to hear us fine. At the hospital, when Baba lifted her from Mama's chest and recited her first call to prayer by her ear, she woke and kicked open her swaddle of pink and blue striped blankets. The Texas Children's nurses marveled at her verve. At home, Mama sang her ditties in Urdu, I chanted Itsy Bitsy Spider. Sana flapped her arms, she cooed.

Mama had the baby's seven-day-old head shaved of the unclean birth hair. Baba weighed the hair, calculated its worth in weight in silver and distributed charity in that amount. Her hair grew back in straight and jet black and oh so thick that Mama wouldn't stop talking about it. I was only four. I hadn't thought to consider the worth of my own head of hair until then.

One weekend, as Mama massaged oil into my wispy strands, I mustered the courage to ask, "Was my baby hair as heavy as Sana's?" I ached for Mama to say that mine was just as precious as the baby's.

She combed harder, as if to tug length from my scalp. "We were too poor for ceremonies when you were born." She cut a clean part, twisting my hair into two taut braids. "We're more blessed now. Your father wanted to thank Allah for that."

Fortune was always on our parents' mind. Baba prayed for it. Mama protected it. She made sure baby Sana bore a black dot of kajal on her temple. "To ward off the evil eye," she explained to me.

Several inquisitive aunties in our apartment complex had the evil eye. In the days before the baby's birth, a cracked clay cooking pot of Mama's, a flat tire on Baba's new halal meat delivery van, and even an "unsatisfactory" on my pre-K report card had been blamed on the aunties' jealous glances.

I wondered if I could summon my own evil eye. To curse the baby. She had better hair than me. I might thwart some other trait.

I stared in the bathroom mirror, the only one in the house, willing my evil eye to emerge. Was it possible that I was too young? I exercised my eyeballs to strengthen them. Sometimes, I stared so long that I lost perspective and my face took on dimensions that scared me so I feared I might have inflicted my nascent evil on myself.

I eyed Sana especially hard in the quarter of an hour after her bath when Mama lay her down on my bed, massaged and diapered her, and reapplied her daily dot. My bed stank of mustard oil for hours afterwards. For this transgression alone, the baby deserved the eye.

A year of effort came to naught: Sana astounded everyone by walking at eleven months instead of the fourteen it had taken me. When she took her first step, Baba happened to be home, just having finished his ablutions for the Friday prayer at the mosque. His hair damp, his sleeves still rolled above the elbow, he picked her up from where she had plopped by the coffee table and twirled her in the air. Sana shrieked with delight.

He'd never spun me that way. I held up my arms. "Me too, Baba!"

He dropped Sana on the sofa, unrolled his sleeves and buttoned them. "Can't you see you're too big?"

I couldn't tell whether he meant too old or too large for our crammed living room. From the firmness of Mama's hand on my shoulder, I understood not to repeat my request or ask why. I was a part of the setting, Sana the shiny new thing.

Mama picked up the baby and beamed at Baba. "Masha'Allah."

Baba rested his hand on Sana's head. "May she walk far in life."

Baba saw a good omen in Sana's early steps. He wanted to give thanks in the proper way and have a goat slaughtered in her name via the sadqah service at the mosque.

But the mosque's administrative offices were closed in observance of the Friday holy day. After Baba returned to his shop, Juan, his butcher, argued with him that the mosque charged retail for sacrifices and convinced him to use one of their own wholesale goats. So Baba dedicated to Sana the first goat that arrived in his Saturday shipment and distributed shares of it to our neighbors. He arrived home anxious with doubt about whether he'd done the right thing by listening to a Catholic man—whether the charity of a goat dedicated post-slaughter would count. Mama, who appreciated Juan's good sense with finances, reminded Baba that Catholics were the closest to Muslims out of all Christians. And hadn't they named me Mariam?

She set Baba at ease so that, by dinnertime, he was in a celebratory mood again. He told his old funny story of how he'd come here, how he'd gotten called in the green card lottery at the same time as another Fazal from Pakistan, and how that man's wife, now a widow, Ghazala, had been certain the fates would never allow it, had berated her husband for bringing the green card lottery to Baba's attention. Then he talked of the restaurant his shop would expand into. "What do you think, Huma, will Ghazala Apa come to eat at our restaurant?"

"Uff," Mama said, feigning high drama. "She lives one intersection down from us and has never visited our house—because she's an elder, and we should be the one's visiting her. Maybe her son will pick up some takeout for her."

I laughed with Mama and Baba, reveling in their shared joy, a rare sight for me. Most days, they walked with strained shoulders, strategizing, each in their own way, how we were going to make the most of the little bounties that had trickled in this month, how we might stretch them to the next year.

By the time Sana turned three, I was certain my ill intentions had no power.

On a birthday trip to the dollar store, I had chosen a bubblegum-pink photo album with two-by-two grids. Side-by-side, I slid in pictures of Sana and me as newborns. My collection grew into an age-matched pairing of photographs of the two of us. She was not only prettier than me at every stage but glowed as if she harbored so much life her image would leap off the paper.

To shake me out of my obsessed comparisons, Mama assigned me a hundred small tasks to help out with Sana. I did them to please Mama. But, so far, it had taken all my self-control not to topple her over on her diapered butt.

One day, as I worked on my album on the bedroom floor, tucking in a picture of Sana cutting her third birthday cake, Mama sat next to me. "She's going to need you."

I tingled with the premonition that I had something Sana did not. "I'll help you, Mama."

"Not me. You have to help her." Mama took both my hands in hers. "She can't talk."

"She's little."

"You were talking by your first birthday."

I remained silent, afraid to ask Mama anything, terrified I might divulge my evil eye to her. I was confused. I talked with Sana all the time. I understood her when she spoke back—babbled back, signed back. Wasn't that how toddlers spoke?

As soon as I was alone, I flipped to our pictures from our first birthdays. The two of us looked more similar than I remembered. What had I hoped to steal from Sana? Surely, not her words. *Sana the walker*, I told myself, *Mariam the talker*.

Mama didn't have much faith in doctors, and definitely no patience for what some of our more fashionable acquaintances, like Noreen Auntie who lived in a gated townhome community inside the loop, dropped hints about: therapists. We had no pediatrician. Mama ushered us in and out of the nurses' station for our regimen of shots. She slid the refreshed immunization records into the same manila envelope as the previous ones, never discarding the historical copies. The envelope sat in a stern gray SentrySafe with other legal paperwork and Mama's wedding gold. Other than our shots, we battled every ailment with cayenne-laced chicken broth and in the wintertime, relieved our phlegm-clogged lungs in a steamy bathroom while Mama held us in her lap and chanted her way through Dr. Seuss books.

"White-people black magic," Baba said, whenever he caught her reading Dr. Seuss to us.

Mama ignored Baba's grumbling and spent our toy budget on the books. Sana would tap along to the rhythms of her reading. "Rhyming sounds are good for them," Mama informed Baba.

By the time I grew out of those books, I had a sense that Mama also thought those books were white-people witchery, but she wanted her children to imbibe that magic.

Baba ceded the raising of us to Mama and our school. He left for his shop on the desi strip at seven AM, and returned smelling of used cardboard boxes at nine PM. Most families in our apartment complex were Pakistani. The common lounge served as the hosting place for birthday parties and potluck Ramadan iftaars, as well as the de facto weekday mosque for the menfolk. Baba showered and headed there for his nighttime prayer, and to make up any of the other four he might have missed.

In the days after Mama told me about Sana, Baba stayed later at his prayers. It was as if the good fortune he had seen in Sana had been a delusion. Even on weekends, we spoke less to each other. Baba walked more slowly, with the weight of long years ahead of him. At his shop, Baba squeezed out every bit of profit by buying the cheapest animals he could wrestle from the halal slaughterhouses with the cleanest trucks, only giving Juan his first raise the year he got married.

Juan had wandered into our apartment complex looking for a place, assuming he was in the one with the Hispanic community. Baba pointed him across the street, then asked him if he was legal and whether he needed a job. In addition to his pay, Juan took home half the meat they couldn't sell in time.

Baba brought home the other half. Mama cooked up the meat the next morning into a watery gravy with potatoes and charged the university boys who roomed together in the complex three dollars a meal. The boys had to eat halal. They hated the steamed fish and broccoli on campus, so they were thankful for her catering. I enjoyed walking with Mama to deliver the aloo gosht to the boys. She came alive on those errands, casting her motherliness over them as if she had endless stores. She asked after their classes and news of their families. I'd help by carrying a Tupperware container in both hands and waited for one of the boys to take it from me appreciatively. When he handed me the payment, I passed it to Mama with pride, as if I'd earned it.

Mama brought us money in another way too. The first weekend of April felt like a festival in our home. Mama invited Juan and regaled him with goat biryani and carrot halwa until the accounts had been sorted and the paperwork organized in shoeboxes she'd held on to. Baba then took him out for strong brewed chai down the road. They escaped the apartment as put-upon brothers needing air, out of the clutches of woman.

Later that week, Mama accompanied Baba to drive the boxes to Saqlain Uncle's Al-Adnan Tax & Insurance Agency & Notary. We were the only household in the complex to receive a significant refund check from the IRS every year. The other women muttered about the legality of Mama's maneuverings when the check manifested as lace-edged sofa slipcovers, a new microwave oven, a family flight to Lahore for a cousin's wedding. Mama would shut them up with, "Who's stopping you all from seeing Saqlain Bhai?"

At least, when it came to Sana, the aunties were kindhearted. They offered her hand-me-down stuffed toys. At the playground behind the complex, they yelled at their kids to let her go first on the slides. I got my fair share of these scoldings for being less than attentive to her. I wasn't ashamed. The rudimentary sign language that was blossoming at home had spread to the neighborhood children. Sana clambered like a cat on the jungle gym I'd fallen from as a toddler and avoided ever since. She didn't need my help on the playground. Playgrounds don't need words; only a sense of one's body and others' bodies.

The aunties' encouragement of Sana lasted until it came time for her enrollment in kindergarten. The two neighbors also registering their kids that summer saw Mama in the school line. They showed up at our place at teatime. As Mama fried up samosas from her freezer, they followed her into the kitchen, protesting that she shouldn't go to such lengths, that they'd only come out of concern for poor Sana. In the living room, I turned down the TV volume to eavesdrop. Sana sensed my unease. She straightened up too. The women were trying to convince Mama that Sana should be homeschooled.

"Besides," said Nuzhat Auntie, "being a fortunate mother of four sons, but also the mother of a daughter, I'm telling you she's going to have a hard time when she's grown. She might as well be used to the safety of home."

Kinza Auntie spoke in a pleading tone about how back home shame was kept behind curtains, how she was saying this for Mama's own good. She paused, then added, "And think of the embarrassment to Mariam at school."

My ears burned at the idea that my sister might be an embarrassment to anyone, to our family, to me. I turned the volume up, as much to drown out my own thoughts as the women's voices. But Sana snatched the remote from me and turned it down again. The women remained in the kitchen, teaspoons tinkling in cups, samosas crunched right after being ladled from the kadhai.

Nuzhat Auntie asked Mama if there was any more mint raita, then proceeded to look herself—her voice sounded as if her head was in the fridge. "You think the teachers will bother with her?"

The fridge door slammed shut. "If they don't, I will sue them." Mama's voice was syrupy cold like the cloying rosewater and screw pine drink the aunties poured for us on summer afternoons. They left.

Sue. Another American word that intimidated the folks in the complex. Mama knew enough such words to get what she needed. By the time Sana started school, I was already a weary veteran of Mama's lack of subtlety in these matters. She strove to acquire a vocabulary of rights and used what she garnered like a fire hose.

The week before school, Mama made four copies of a letter. One was addressed to the principal, the other to the social worker, one to the school nurse, and one to Sana's as-yet-unassigned homeroom teacher. The letter said that Sana should be provided a special education teacher under the Individuals with Disabilities Education Act, and that we would sue the school if she wasn't.

Baba had to get the copies notarized at Saqlain Uncle's agency. "What was the need, Huma?" He threw the letters on the kitchen counter when he returned. "Saqlain did it, but he had that amused look on his face the whole time."

"Why should we care what others think?"

"His child is in school with Mariam. They're a good family with a good business."

Mama glanced at me but said nothing. Baba was talking about Saqlain Uncle's son, Adnan. I assumed Baba meant that I was in academic competition with him. Later, I would realize that their interest in Adnan and his prospects included a possible future for me. Adnan had two older brothers and a little sister the same age as Sana. Our parents made sure to attend to Saqlain Uncle's family at community gatherings. We had scant excuse to visit with them otherwise. I couldn't be expected to play with the boys, and they didn't want Sana to be left alone with the girl. Children can be cruel; Amal was known to be particularly high spirited.

On the first day of fourth grade, Mama brought me with her to the principal's office at our K-12 charter school. Just that morning I had tried to tell her that Sana would be okay, that there were other kids who worked with a special-ed teacher.

"And do you think those children just walked into that special class?" Mama held my eyes until I had to look away, the way she did when she wanted me to remember a life lesson.

She handed the principal her letters, tucked into the manila envelope that usually held our shot records, and reminded him that we were an established PTA-dues-paying family. The principal knew Mama well by now. He winked at me, as if he and I were on the same team. He graciously accepted the documents and told Mama he would do his best to spare her the trouble of a lawsuit. I was mortified.

Afterwards, as I buckled myself into our overheated car, I threw Sana, sweaty in the booster seat she was too big for, the kind of hard evil eye I hadn't in months. School hadn't begun and already she'd put me in an awkward spot. I recalled Kinza Auntie's concern for me. I worried that if I was too helpful to Sana at school, others might see me the way the principal had seen Mama—overprotective, untrusting.

Come September, Sana's schedule included three days a week of pullout classes with a special-ed teacher. Other than that, she passed me in the hallways like any other kid, waving back if I waved at her, and, to my relief, looking away if I chose not to make eye contact.

A month into school, as our parents waited to break their day-long Ramadan fast at our four-person white plastic dining table, Sana tried to sign with us. She used the ASL from school. She wanted to get the grownups' attention, so I held still. Mama cocked her head, trying to follow. Baba did nothing.

When Sana tried again, her eyes flashing with anticipation, Baba sighed. "What's this now?"

I didn't follow ASL yet, but I've always known Sana's thoughts. "She's asking you to pass her the watermelon." I was speaking and simultaneously signing in our homegrown language. He'd had years to get used to that.

Mama chuckled to break the tension. "You girls are old enough now to wait with us till the sun sets. Three minutes to go."

As soon as Mama and Baba had broken their fast with a date and a sip of lemonade, Sana, bouncing in her seat, signed again for the watermelon. Mama smiled and copied her deliberately, making eye contact with Baba. Silently, she was pleading with him to try as well. He wouldn't. I reached across the table and passed the watermelon to Sana. Mama then asked Sana the sign for lemonade. I was surprised she did, because Baba's arms were crossed. Even I knew that meant he wanted things to end right there. This wasn't like his complaints about our picture books.

Across from him, Sana sat with her arms folded too. She only budged when Mama asked her how to say lemonade a second time. Soon, Mama, Sana and I were passing food around the table as if it were a game. Sana and I were giggling, then laughing hard as we got faster. We got so speedy that as I reached across the table, I knocked over Baba's lemonade, splashing him.

He pushed away from the table. Melamine bowls brimming with chaat and pakoras clattered together. The tamarind chutney spilled and muddied the puddle of lemonade.

"Can a man not be at home even within his own four walls?" He stormed off.

Sana stared after him.

I searched Mama's distraught face. I had caused the accident, but Mama looked as if it had been her fault.

She jumped up, startling us. "Stop this nonsense!"

"You were playing with us, too!" My voice shook. I'd ruined Baba's clothes. Baba had ruined Sana's accomplishment.

"Just eat," Mama said, her voice lower. "I have to find him a clean outfit."

As the door to their room closed, Sana's face scrunched as if she was about to cry. When I scrunched my face too, echoing her pain, she took a deep breath—the way Mama had been teaching her to take control rather than crumble into a tantrum—and told me, "Baba doesn't want me."

"Of course he does!" She had no memory of his celebrations in her name, the blessings he'd cast on her, how he'd prayed she would walk far in life.

"Also Mama doesn't want me," she insisted. "She wants Baba."

"She wants both of you. I promise. Talk to her in the morning."

Sana and I lay listening as our parents fought in their room. Baba accused Mama of encouraging Sana's non-communicative behavior. Mama screamed about his indifference to her efforts. Baba missed both his sundown and his nighttime prayers.

He didn't like unpredictability. He had been upset when Juan's wife left him without an explanation. "The least a hardworking decent man like that deserves is a comfortable home and a committed wife," he proclaimed for days. That was the second time he gave Juan a raise. That night, as our parents argued, I suspected Baba needed to be sure that Mama wouldn't leave him the way Juan's wife had left.

The next morning, even though we were running late for school, Sana signed in ASL that she wanted to lace up her shoes herself.

Mama continued to tie her laces grimly. "Save your American Sign Language for your American school."

Sana met my eyes, reminding me of my promise that Mama was on her side too. I grabbed her hand and ran for the bus.

Halfway there, she shook my hand off.

SANA STOPPED TRYING. To our homemade sign language, she added a few new words, the bare essentials of puberty and adolescence: pads, allowance, calculator, deodorant. Mama continued putting her signature on Sana's school forms. I selected ASL as my second language in middle school and Mama didn't comment when I brought home my first report card.

Still, I grumbled about Sana's A's every now and then. When Mama gloated over her flawless math scores in sixth grade, I told her, "I could do that too if I got all those special accommodations and extra time on my tests."

"Allah has given you enough special accommodations," Mama snapped at me, "so make use of those first."

I did. I told myself I was setting Sana an example. The truth was, I wouldn't be able to stand it if she did better than me, considering. I could hear what the aunties would say. And by high school, I had another incentive. Adnan was in the same grade as me and was acing his AP classes.

Baba had never needed to tell me, but I knew that, like other girls in our circles, I wasn't supposed to talk to boys. None of our mothers had male acquaintances. At public gatherings, only married couples socialized with other married couples. At school, simply making eye contact or saying hi to Adnan felt like a subversive act, even though Baba was fond of him. Over time, Adnan and I found transactional reasons to talk at school—nothing we wouldn't be able to back up academically. Our shared glances lingered longer. We formed friend groups that met in public places. We didn't speak to each other in front of our parents.

I did get guilty satisfaction out of two things. In middle school, Sana's trophies for music and art had begun to crowd our living room tables along with Mama's glass and ceramic trinkets. Once, Baba set his teacup down and knocked over a blown glass elephant. As Mama gathered the body and the trunk and the tail into her dupatta, Baba waved at the cluttered side table. "What good are these for her future?"

Mama said nothing, but in the coming days she relocated Sana's trophies to a decorative shelf in our bedroom. By the end of that school year, Sana moved the trophies to her closet, and placed any new ones she received in there as well.

Only my framed honor roll certificates graced the living room now, no matter how old they got.

By the time I was in high school, Mama, out of habit, still sent me to deliver the aloo gosht curry to the university boys. As I'd grown up, the boys were closer to me in age, every year a fresh face or two. I, of course, looked forward to the errand and lingered. The day I was gone over fifteen minutes, Mama lost patience for my excuse of "they didn't answer the door for really long." She reassigned my chore to Sana who, she assumed, would not chat up the boys. I chafed at the unfairness of it. But when I asked Sana what the boys said to her, she told me they barely said "hello" or "thank you." I acknowledged a twinge of pleasure.

However, this joy was to be short lived. By the fall of Sana's eighth grade, she brought home a letter from school for a weekend field trip to San Antonio, where bands from around the state were competing. I had never been allowed on out-of-town trips. All I attended were the half-day visits to the museums, to which we were supposed to bring sack lunches and somehow my parents never figured out the thing about decent brown paper bags and stuck me with the plastic Thank You bag from Baba's shop.

"Why didn't you just say no, like you do with the older one?" Baba snapped as I moped over dinner.

Sana was in San Antonio. I pushed my food around my plate, picturing her in some hotel hallway having a pillow fight with her classmates.

Mama told me to eat properly, then mumbled in Baba's direction. "I was afraid if I didn't sign her papers, they'd say I wasn't supporting her special education."

"What does this have to do with her special education?"

"I don't know." Her face looked old for the first time. "They told me music class is part of her therapy."

"*You* don't know?" Baba laughed as if he had been relieved of some burden. "And how much did this cost us, two hundred dollars? Three hundred? Can they force us to pay that?"

Mama's fire of old flushed back to her face. She served him more eggplant bharta. "Not one cent, I tell you. What do you think? I know the boxes to check on those papers."

Mama's only relief in letting Sana go on those increasingly frequent trips was that none of the aunties had anything too vicious to say about it. Sana was not an eligible future wife for any of their sons.

Then came the day that I saw Sana signing with a boy in the school hallway. As I helped Mama in the kitchen that night, I mentioned that Sana had found a homework friend at school.

"Good." Mama passed me a dirty knife. "She should bring her home some time."

"It's a boy." I washed the knife. "Dylan."

Mama paused mid-stir. "Are you telling me your sister is talking to boys at school now?"

I considered and set the knife down to dry. "Not exactly."

We left it at that. Mama had heard me. But the matter of socializing with boys, it turned out, was as nuanced as the matter of field trips.

Sana and Dylan walked together down school hallways. On the days Sana stayed back because her band was performing at a game, I would pick her up because Mama detested driving at night. I didn't tell Mama that Sana and Dylan sat apart from the rest of the band. My heart pounded when I saw them holding hands. I couldn't decide if it was out of excitement for Sana, or resentment because I had never dared to hold Adnan's hand in school, hold my face so close to his that we might feel each other's breath.

In my senior year at the University of Houston, Sana got into Bard. Her guidance counselor and special ed teacher had helped her apply to multiple schools on music scholarships.

"Aren't you glad you did your taxes?" Mama asked Baba at the table the day we heard that Sana had gotten a full ride.

I almost blurted out that Dylan had gotten a full ride to Bard too. But Sana made eye contact with me just then. I let it go. After all, Adnan was at UH with me.

He'd been accepted into UT Austin. But spring break of senior year in high school, we sneaked over to Galveston with our friend groups, where he told me how his dad had begged him to stay in Houston to help with the agency, how his older brothers had no interest in the family business. I felt sorry for Adnan. He was so different from his blustering father. He protected his sister from his parents' wrath and had this gentle manner with me that I couldn't imagine evolving into our fathers' egos with their women. I had begun to think of him as not just my boyfriend but my man. So, when he asked me at the beach what he should do, I thought of myself, then answered with a kiss to help him make up his mind.

Sana was aware of how much time Adnan and I spent together in college. She and I still shared our bedroom. Baba had not allowed me to move to the dorms.

Baba's arms were crossed again that night at the table as we talked about Bard. He glanced at Mama. "So, you're sending her?"

"I'm going," Sana signed. "No one is sending me."

Baba looked to me for an explanation, as he had over the last decade when something pressing had to be clarified between them.

I shifted in my seat. "She's going."

"I know she said that. What else?"

"No one is sending me," Sana repeated.

I sighed. "No one is sending her."

"Please." Mama sounded tired. "Stop it, girls."

Baba got up from the table. So did Sana.

"You think you can leave, just like that?" Baba's voice was low, controlled.

They stood there, the two of them. She had grown almost as tall as him. She'd shot past Mama, and then me, years ago. I had not thought to compare her to Baba.

"I'm eighteen," she told him, looking him straight in the eye, her mouth firm. He didn't need that interpreted.

Baba glared at Mama. "And leaving is her right in this country, isn't it?" She didn't look up at him. He thumped the table in front of her. "Isn't it?"

Mama glanced at Sana, then Baba. "Why are you asking me, Fazal? Ask her."

SANA WAS AWAY on a post-college internship in Milan when I messaged her about my wedding. Baba had asked us what her summer plans were after her freshman year, and never asked again. He did not fight fights he couldn't win.

Sana skipped my pre-wedding henna ceremony that was hosted at the community center in our apartment complex, catered by Juan who now managed the cafeteria Baba's shop had expanded into. Thank goodness Saqlain Uncle had business connections with one of the best hotels in Sugar Land so at least our wedding reception would be something to remember.

Mama wouldn't touch the gold at the desi jewelers on Hillcroft, dismissing their patterns as decades old. She had my trousseau and jewelry made in Pakistan and flown in by Baba's sister.

Adnan's mother's dresses caused a minor scandal with their grandeur. The aunties who had seen them ahead of time hinted to Mama that the mother-in-law was competing with the bride.

"Let her be." Mama waved them off. "The foolish woman will draw the evil eye to herself, as if she needs anymore. Her older sons are still single, and she's suffered enough heartache from that runaway daughter of hers."

The day before the wedding, I met Sana and Dylan for brunch at their hotel in downtown. Sana handed me a print of her engagement picture. "For your album." She grinned.

She'd found my album when I was in high school and teased me about it, so I stopped using it. But before she left for Bard, she gave me a print of her high school graduation photo. We slid it into the album together, along with one of mine, which we snuck from Mama's collection in a shoebox she kept on top of the SentrySafe.

I took in the photo and swallowed. A pinched sensation buried away for many years stirred up again. I forced a laugh. "You look happier in yours."

My engagement had been a formal community affair, I weighed down by layers as heavy as a bridal outfit, Adnan in a suit and tie too stuffy for that humid Houston summer. Sana and Dylan got engaged in linen, on a breezy spring day at a farm in the Hudson Valley.

The next evening, Sana arrived at the door of the bridal suite at the wedding hotel hand in hand with Dylan. Mama was tucking a string of jasmines into my braid.

When Sana introduced Dylan as her fiancé, Mama glanced at me, at a loss for words. The other women in the room averted their eyes, giving Mama some dignified space. Mama continued to adorn my hair. Sana and Dylan waited.

Mama pinned the last jasmine by my ear, poking a bit harder. "Did you know this, Mariam?"

I couldn't reply because Nuzhat Auntie's daughter, who was now a sought-after desi makeup artist, was daubing a new layer of lipstick on me. Mama had chosen to maintain a silence once. So, I did the same.

Baba was welcoming guests in the men's section. Sana and I knew he would have to host her fiancé as an attendee from the girl's side. If he was angry, he wouldn't be able to show it. There was my future to think of; Saqlain Uncle's reputation to maintain.

Mama understood all this too, but her face burned for Baba. She beckoned Dylan. "Follow me." She would walk him to Baba herself.

Dylan threw Sana an apprehensive glance. She nodded at him reassuringly. Mama would know what to do.

As soon as Mama returned, Sana asked her what she'd told Baba. She'd been on edge after all.

Mama slid my veil off its hanger. "I reminded him that Saqlain Bhai has had his own daughter's shame to deal with." As she rifled through the box of safety pins, she told us that Baba had shaken Dylan's hand and introduced him to Juan, tasking Juan with making sure that he was well fed.

Then she spun toward Sana. "Why would you do this to me for some—just some boy? After everything I've done for you?"

Sana met my eyes. Mama had exerted what power she had to open doors for Sana, but she'd also chosen to close others behind her. Sana adjusted her perfectly pleated sari.

"He speaks my tongue," she said, in our childhood family signs.

Mehr

Mehr perched on the crescent moon at the tip of the minaret of the town mosque. It was almost noon. She had lingered there since the call to prayer rang out before dawn. She stretched her wings and settled down once more to watch the bustle on the platform of the torn-up train station below, looking for one man.

Harried workers on their way to brick factories stumbled into rusted cars, one of them dragging his teenaged boy behind him. Mehr used to play with the boy, until his mother began to shoo her away, telling them it wasn't proper anymore. Another train, from the direction of the farming villages, squealed into the opposite track. Women alighted from its cars and drifted into the market—women in blue burqas and black, in durable chaddars, in diaphanous dupattas, women with children trailing behind, with husbands striding ahead.

In another life, Mehr thought, her mother might have been among them. Back in the village they said that the dust of Sianapur had killed her; that she was never meant to toil among the hawkers and sweepers who scraped a living off this station; that when she was a girl, her feet barely touched the earth as she raced through the fields. Her family had begged her to raise Mehr in the clean air of her ancestral village. But her husband Mirza, an absconded musician, a man who had come from Lahore searching for a bride, a crazed look in his eyes but a small fortune in his pockets, would not let his wife, and then their daughter out of his sight. He knew how the child took after her mother. He took them to Sianapur and set up as an instrument repairman. But this was a town of trucks, not tablas.

A flutter by the snack stall of the train station caught Mehr's eye. She spied her father, now a struggling truck mechanic who had sunk his savings into a craft he had never been able to master. He spun away from the counter, despondent, his grease-stained tunic still wrinkled from having been slept in. Moeen, the stall owner, followed him a short way, handed him a cone of roasted peanuts and a gingery cup of sugarcane juice and gruffly refused payment. Mehr cocked her head and followed her father's movements around the bazaar in the alleys behind the station. Mirza did not stop to sift through a jumble of spare parts or search his pockets for change to indulge in a tobacco-laced betel leaf paan. No, he was looking for something. For someone.

Leaping off the minaret, Mehr splayed her wings, circled the mosque a few times and coasted down to the bazaar. She raised her wings to descend toward her father. He caught her approach from the corner of his eye and threw his forearms up to shield his face. Of course, he didn't recognize her. She had told him as much. She couldn't resist scraping his arm with a talon and when he swatted her away in fright, she circled over him and approached a few more times, angling away just as he lifted his arms.

Amusing as she found this new game, Mehr stopped harassing him and retreated to settle on the roof of the train station to continue to watch his futile search.

TWO WEEKS AGO, Mehr's father had come home to their one-room flat on the rooftop of a tenement on the edge of town and held out a taped-up paper bag.

"What is it, Abba?" She skipped up to him barefoot across the cement floor, snatching a rare gift from his hands.

"Why won't you wear your chappals around the room, Mehr?"

He had begun to be more impatient with her of late. She paid mind to the tape instead of him. "I'm not going to catch a cold."

"Yes, but your feet are going to crack and look like an old woman's and then how will I find a boy for you?"

Another time, she would have told him to keep his boys busy in his truck repair shop; twist their ears to focus on their job so he wouldn't lose so much money. They would quibble over his inexplicable obsession with training that urchin, Chhota, who was too young to learn the tools and would rather fritter away his day thieving from train passengers.

But she was too enchanted to nag him. Sliding her hand into the bag, she lingered on the ethereal silkiness between her fingers, holding off the revelation for a few more moments. Her life was rarely one of soft things. "It's so light."

When she eased the fabric out, a black burqa spilled open in her hands. A jolt ran down her spine. The dread of that moment, she had anticipated, but it was the thrill that jarred her.

"Mehr, my beti, it is time. You are now…you look—"

"What, Abba?" She knew he would find the scorn in her voice irritating—scorn he had invited for not flatly saying what he meant. She flung open the chest in which she kept her knickknacks and with a pinch in her heart and an aggrieved eye cast at her father, threw the burqa in with her dusty rag dolls.

"This was not from the station bazaar, Mehr! I saved and went to the city. It belongs in your cupboard, not in that toy box."

"The cupboard already has one in it—Ammi's."

"I thought you might prefer your own. The women in the bazaar talk about this lighter fabric the college girls wear in the city." His voice sank. "Your Ammi's was so heavy."

When Mehr said nothing, he tried again. "We both lost her that day, Mehr. Don't think I don't know your pain."

"I lost her once before too, Abba," Mehr said, grabbing her mother's burqa from the cupboard. She threw it over herself, pulling the headpiece down tight over her face so that her voice was muffled. "I was five. She was wearing this at the station in Lahore. We'd gone all the way looking for you when you'd taken your tablas again and hadn't returned for two nights." She twisted the fabric under her chin so that her face flushed hot with the trapped blood. "Ammi let go of my hand to pick up our basket— and disappeared."

Her father grabbed her wrist and squeezed it until she relaxed the vise. "Just because you couldn't spot her doesn't mean she'd abandoned you."

"It was a field of mothers."

"You are here now."

Mehr inserted all five fingers into the face-net of her mother's burqa and yanked it off, flinging it to her father's feet.

She imagined that if he were any other father, she might not have lived to see another morning in his house. Another father in his position, at his most merciful, might have dragged her by the hair to her grandmother's house, no matter how far, and ordered that she be married off to the first man they could find.

But in this home, they only had each other.

Her father lowered himself onto his cot and lay down. He covered his eyes with a pillow and muttered, "You have the shape of a woman now, Mehr. If your mother were here, maybe she could have taught you to talk like one too."

"I thought the burqa was supposed to stop me from talking to people."

He said nothing.

"You know I can't stand not to talk," she pattered on. "You complain about that everyday yourself."

He sat up. "And are all the other burqa-clad ladies on the street mute? Do they not get their business done?"

She had no answer. She only knew that once she donned it, she would become a thing both expected and unknown. A thing without a will, she imagined.

"The boys and men are looking at you now, beti," her father said, with some embarrassment. "You must protect yourself from their gaze."

She was not unaware that her honor was his honor. She tried, for the most part, to not be a disgrace to him. But it felt as if, from this moment on, his honor required her to cease to be.

"And if I put it on, how will you know your own daughter from the other creatures floating down the street?"

"A father knows his own daughter." He got up and left the room, muttering about the inconvenience of a dead wife.

The following weekend, Mehr met her cousin at the train station. She would have missed her if Shama hadn't called out as she descended from the train, newly burqa-clad. Her mother stepped down behind her. Mehr thought her aunt's embrace held more pity for her than usual. After all, not only was Mehr motherless, but in a week, would become the unmarried cousin. Though only fifteen, Shama was in town on the fortunate errand of collecting her wedding dress from the tailor.

As they wove through the bazaar toward the tailor's workshop, the girls several steps ahead of the woman, the shopkeepers announced their wares to them in a way they never did to Mehr. *They know me too well, that's why,* Mehr told herself. But she sensed an arch in Shama's movements whenever they were addressed. Both girls knew it was Shama they summoned.

When they arrived at their favorite bangle stall, Shama grabbed Mehr's hand and swung her past the sparkling rows upfront. With a nod from her mother, who stopped to browse the bangles, she pulled Mehr into the long narrow room behind the stall to look at the jewelry too special to display to mere passersby.

"Is your dress ready?" Shama asked Mehr, fingering a pair of dangling earrings in silver and turquoise.

"I still have the borders of the dupatta to finish." She had been embroidering the outfit for a month now.

"All in silver thread?"

"You said it should be. You said only silver would do on that midnight blue?"

"Good," Shama said. "Imagine us together Meeri—my gold and pink next to your silver and blue." She squeezed Mehr's hand. "You will be spoken for the instant we enter the room."

Mehr, aching to squeeze Shama's hand back, snatched hers away instead and lowered her voice. "How can I picture it? You're hiding from me under this new thing."

"Oh, hush," Shama whispered and handed the earrings to the shopkeeper. "Here, Ammi said I was to buy these for you for the wedding. Mirza Uncle won't think of such things."

When Shama emerged from behind the seamstress's curtain, resplendent, Mehr wanted to reach for her cheek and pinch it gently into a blush the way they used to when they played at brides. But the seamstress and the mother crowded Shama, cooing and inspecting the bride-to-be from every angle until they were satisfied.

Mehr watched the seamstress fold the pink silk and chiffon in layer upon layer of muslin so the embroidery would not snag on itself. Shama finally emerged from behind the curtain, petulant that it had taken her a while to adjust her burqa, giggling when her mother said she would be used to it soon enough.

As the train pulled into the station, the girls hung back as Shama's mother kept an eye on their acquisitions.

"Meeri? Come with me." Shama begged a final time. "It's our last week!"

"Abbu needs me here," Mehr said. In fact, she had never asked her father if she could spend the week before the wedding with Shama. They had only exchanged hems and grunts since the day of the burqa.

"I need you!"

"No, you don't," Mehr said, flicking at Shama's burqa.

"Why do you hate it?"

"It's taken you from me."

Shama checked to see if her mother was looking and then lowered her voice. "You saw me today."

How could Mehr tell her how it felt to see her for only those fleeting moments when she had shimmered into view in the seamstress' room?

"If you come today," Shama whispered, "I will tell you how it feels."

"To disappear?" Mehr hissed back.

"To only appear," Shama said as the train screeched into the station and her mother called to her to hurry, "to those you want."

Those words had a pull on Mehr that felt physical; from when they were little, Shama had always been able to tempt her into anything. But on this day, Mehr saw past their game of the moment. "What about after the wedding?" Mehr said. "You'll leave for your husband's home, and I'll have to come back here."

Shama huffed. "I'll have responsibilities, won't I?" Her voice had the tinge of a scold, a tone that Mehr had only heard before in her aunt's voice. "Besides, he spoke to my father of America, Meeri. Can you imagine? Not Lahore. Not Dubai. All the way to Houston?"

"They say he's frail as a straw of hay," Mehr blurted, bile in her throat. When Shama's shoulders slumped, she took the hand of the only sister she had ever known. "Oh Shama, I hope he's carried away by foul winds if he steals you so far away from me. You belong here and nowhere else."

But Shama did not read the pain, the longing in Mehr, heard only a curse in her words. She dropped her hand and, without looking back, stepped onto the train behind her mother.

The night before the wedding, as Mehr had expected, her father refused to take her with him if she would not don the burqa, display the modicum of public modesty he expected from her at this age.

Mehr didn't hide from her father the sound of her bitter tears that night. As much pride as she had, she was not sorry he knew her anguish. In fact, she hoped that he would see the smallness in his insistence. Even on the morning of the wedding, she could not bring herself to cover up under that black tent the sublime outfit she had adorned by hand for a month.

He left without her. He hung up the burqa on a nail by the front door. It was a reminder, he told her, of who remained in charge in that household.

She lay on her cot and stared at the burqa swaying in the slight breeze from their open casement. As the sun traversed the sky, she watched the shadows of the bars in the casement slither across the bare cement floor. At the hour the sun began its descent, she thought the burqa beckoned to her. She got up, feeling hollow-boned from not having eaten all day, and slid the fabric of the burqa between her fingers. It was even lighter than she remembered, as if it had taken on a liminal aspect to tempt her. In one swift motion, she flicked it off the hook and swirled it over herself. Except for the weight of its cap on her head, she had a sense it disappeared, taking her with it.

In this state of lightness, she opened the door and stepped onto the rooftop. Over the ledge, she observed the scrub-pocked hinterland stretching to the river on the horizon, wondering what the creatures of the marsh would make of her. Perhaps her mother was one of them now, she thought. Her father used to point in that general direction when she asked him, as a little girl, where her Ammi had gone.

The afternoon call to prayer rang out from the town mosque. Shama's nikah would be over by now. By the laws that counted, she now belonged to somebody she had never met. Tonight, those who used to matter to her most could not anymore, and she would be given away.

The clatter of the carts of knickknacks setting up at the train station drifted up to Mehr. She flew down the spiral stairwell on the side of their building and into the bazaar, wandering the streets that used to know the sound of her laughter. When the corn lady didn't offer her a stubby cob, and Chhota didn't call out to her to join him in flicking pebbles at the passing cars of a train, she knew this afternoon she was nothing but a pair of dusty sandals.

She got on the first train that pulled up, sliding in behind a woman with a basket of pakoras in newspaper packets. In the crush of boarding, even the brush of a hand on her back or her arm was absorbed by the barrier of the fabric so that the touch lost all sense of intention and caused neither her, nor the accidental toucher, any chagrin. She stopped at the very next station to breath the open air. Swiping a packet of onion pako-ras, she boarded another train heading back, rode past her own station and explored a bazaar of second-hand trinkets two stops down the line. At a jewelry stall she thought she saw a pair of silver earrings so like the ones Shama had bought for her that she was certain her father had discov-ered hers and sold them off. In a rush of rage, she boarded a train back to her own station.

She could not remember a day in her life when no one had offered her anything or told her to get out of the way. All afternoon, people had swerved around her in silence, holding their things and their thoughts to themselves. Nobody asked her who she was or where she came from or where she was going. No one knew whether she belonged, or she didn't. She felt a strange terror and sense of freedom she never imagined could coexist in her; it was as if she stood in the middle of that marshland behind their house and could see in all directions, yet was afraid of what might be behind her. Not even the landlord's children in the flat below looked up as she swept past them up her stairwell.

Inside, she threw open her cupboard. Her embroidered dress and earrings awaited her.

AT THE VILLAGE STATION, other wedding guests stepped off the late afternoon train with Mehr—people here for the mere formality of the evening meal. Relatives who counted had been here since sunrise, if not the night before. If she had come as the two of them had planned, she would have been helping Shama with her final preparations right now, before the walk to the bridal dais.

Nearing the house, the men split off toward a tent, and the women and children headed into the courtyard of the generous bungalow. Mehr snuck into Shama's room behind a group of young girls carrying tambourines and a tabla.

Shama was ready. She laughed when a young aunt from the other side of her family teased her about how many safety pins she might want for her veil; the more pins, the longer it would take to remove later. "I have no say in anything today," Shama told the aunt.

Mehr did not recognize this new, coy tone. Together, they had spent years defying rules both spoken and unspoken. Whether the challenge was stealing gum from an older brother's satchel or wading in muddy irrigated fields, when one of them faltered the other gave her courage, when one of them was afraid she reached for the other's hand.

Mehr waited for Shama to notice her as she lingered by the doorway. The girls drummed and clapped their way through song after song. Shama did not look around; she had eyes only for her mirror. She stopped tapping her fingers to the beat. She even stopped laughing at her aunt's jibes. It was as if her soul were sinking into the mirror. She could only see, only hear herself.

Mehr backed out as quietly as she had appeared. She wove among the children who were trotting between the courtyard and the men's tent where her father was probably resting after countless lunch servings of the goat curry still simmering outdoors in hulking deghs. A few meters from the tent, she paused. No one would have chastised her if she had carried on, but she sensed a line beyond which her presence would become awkward. She would be called *auntie* by some boy her own age, asked who he might call from the tent. She decided there was nobody she wanted to summon. She retraced her short journey that had felt like a voyage, though the village was just down the line from the town.

When she pushed open the door to their flat, the sun clung to the horizon, directly behind her. The shadow falling into the room, although connected to her feet, was strange to her. She had watched that shadow take on the silhouette of a woman over the last five years. Every afternoon she had stood in that doorway and observed herself for a few minutes, her bouncing ponytails giving way to swaying braids and the angles of her body softening into curves. Sometimes, she traced the shadow of her body with the shadow of her finger.

In the burqa, the oblong specter that lay on the floor had no hands. She raised both arms and grasped the door frame. She glanced behind her across the rooftop and then back into the room, unsure which side of the threshold she would rather be on. The rooftop promised crisp air and breath, the room was redolent with a humid, comforting darkness.

Her glance fell to the floor again and she made out in her new shadow a pair of wings. She kept her arms up and walked backward onto the roof. Her new silhouette followed along, becoming more distinct with every step closer to the ledge. A breeze flattened the fine fabric to her back, sewing it up and down her spine, splaying it along the length of her arms past her fingertips; its pressure dissipated any lingering weight out of the top of her head, through her fingers, down her legs, into the ground. As the sun descended, her shadow lengthened, the wings pointed up and her body curved in a clean swoop down to her feet. She had no need to trace these curves—the shape had become one with her, inside and out as she continued backwards.

As she reached the ledge, the sun dipped below the roof and her shadow disappeared. She could not bear it. She knew she must raise herself if she wanted to catch any remaining light. Along with her new wings, Mehr discovered the strength in her legs to leap onto the ledge in a single bound and take off into the dusky sunlight over the hinterland her mother must haunt.

As she watched her father from the roof of the station, Mehr pictured him returning last night to an empty house. He must have rushed back down to scour the slumbering town. He must have found the burqa missing. Mehr hoped that would have frightened him even more. He might not remember what words she had used, but he would know that she had warned him.

His gait was heavy this morning, his shoulders hunched to avoid the touch of others, as if there were more people teeming around him than ever before. When she had swooped away after scratching him, he had shaken his head as if to clear his paranoia.

Sometimes he looked up at a merchant they frequented, as if deciding whether he could share his predicament. The shame of admitting the loss of his daughter would keep him from speaking. At other times he paused as a slighter form in a burqa swirled past him. But she knew that out of decorum, he would never approach one of those forms and inquire whether she was his daughter, Mehr.

Huma and the Birds

Dubai, 1987

Everything was gold and mirrors here in Dubai and loomed over Huma as if she were but a mouse. She didn't wonder what part was real and what wasn't—all of it glittered blindingly. Sometimes, she had to look away from the opulence of her employers' house because it embarrassed her the way nakedness would. To think that Little Mother, her stepmother, had sold her own gold bangles and nose ring to pay the recruiting agent back in Pakistan so Huma could come here to wash marble floors flecked with gold, wipe down gold filigree banisters.

At Huma's new job one bus ride and one flight but many worlds away from Little Mother, she tried her best not to make eye contact with the man of the house, Mr. Suleiman. This was because Madam, Mrs. Suleiman, had told her not to. As the new housemaid, Huma was also not to talk to Fazal, the Pakistani gardener, because Madam said she wasn't a matchmaker, she needed her house taken care of: a ten-room beachfront villa was not for the faint-hearted wife or distracted servant. Madam had learned from her experience with her last four maids, one from Sri Lanka, one from India, and two from Bangladesh. So, Huma was not to leave the house unless transported by the driver to a preapproved location, not to head to the servants' quarters before she was dismissed for the night, not to show up in the kitchen a minute later than six AM, not to make international phone calls more than once a month, not to scold the six children for any reason ever, not to understarch Mr. Suleiman's shirts or robes, not to overstarch Madam's ankle-length gowns, not to clean Mr. Suleiman's study, not to ask who or why, not to overeat, not to cry. She was to note how Teresa, the nanny, was trim and stalwart. Madam thought "Hindi" girls—her designation for those from any part of the Indian subcontinent—could learn from the Filipinas a thing or two about presentability and stoicism.

At night, Huma observed Teresa's beauty routine. They shared a room on one end of the servants' quarters—a single-story whitewashed concrete structure that stood behind the villa, beyond the lawns and the swimming pool. Adjoining their bedroom were three other rooms: a grill-windowed enclosure with a rusted padlock; next to that, a room into which Nadir, the Egyptian cook, lugged buckets of desiccated limes, sacks of flour and rice, drums of oils and beans, tubs of olives—a room to which only he had been given the key by Madam; and at the far end of the quarters stood an afterthought of a cement-floored bathroom with an unenclosed shower and a squatting toilet.

The walls on Teresa's side of their room were decorated with a diamond-patterned woven sheet her aunt had sent along with her, and posters of pop stars with tall, gelled hair and heavy eyeliner. The dresser with a small mirror was understood to be Teresa's.

Huma folded her clothes into her suitcase and set on her bed's headboard a comb and a taped-up picture of Little Mother. Her stepbrother, Laiq, had snatched it from her suitcase and she'd had to tear it out of his clutches. She'd been hiding from him the oldest picture in the house: a creased black and white of Little Mother holding her as an infant. In the absence of a father, Laiq, a wildfire of a boy, untamable even by their storm of mother, had been lured by the doddering village maulvi to join his madrassah at the mosque. Ridding their home of images had become the boy's first religious obsession and manly act over his mother and sister.

Teresa had no family photos on top of her dresser. Instead, she kept a cassette player and a dozen cassette tapes neatened into a brick, fanned out her Billboard magazines, and arranged in a circle, like dolls at a wedding of toys, a bottle of Dettol antiseptic and one of Vatika hair oil, a jar of Ponds cold cream and a tube of Fair & Lovely neatly squeezed from the bottom up.

"You're prettier than me, I know," Teresa told Huma one night. Her tone was dismissive.

Huma was leaning on her elbow, watching. It was clear to them both that Huma's rosier skin and round dimpled cheeks did not equal sophistication and charm. Teresa showed sleek legs beneath skirts that Huma would never trade her shalwars for. Teresa was the stuff of her magazines, Huma thought, when she secretly flipped through them to keep up with her English.

The household staff all spoke in English, no matter how broken or variously accented. Madam wanted the children to learn. She was the only one allowed to speak to them in Arabic. Their father rarely spoke to them anyway, and when he did, his kudos and his admonitions came naturally in English, both modes of interaction honed on his subordinates at the bank.

Huma had excelled in her English class until her tenth-grade matriculation. Two years later, when a recruiting agent came by the village tea shop pawning opportunities in Dubai, she saw a way out of their poverty. She spoke to him without first asking Little Mother.

A gilded cage they're luring you young people into, Little Mother had warned, when Huma had told her later. *Nobody ever admires wings without also imagining how to clip them.* But the agent had said that this was the 1980s and Dubai was going to be the center of the world, that Dubai valued people like Huma; needed them, in fact.

In her boldness, Huma had told the agent that she was also comfortable with Arabic and could work in the home of a local Emirati family if needed. How hard could daily Arabic be, after all? It shared a script with Urdu. She'd been able to memorize long passages of the Quran even though Little Mother did not keep a copy at home and did not pray. But Huma had heard the boys reciting the verses along with the maulvi. The girls were not taught at the mosque because it would be a distraction to the boys. So, she'd taught herself the sounds though she had no one to reveal to her the meanings. Did she discover any masculine magic, acquire any patriarchal powers? Nothing she could point to, but perhaps the strength was in the speaking. Certainly, reciting the verses to herself put her in a trance—perhaps one day she might be able to harness their blessings as well. Other than the boys' time at the mosque, there was no other difference she could see between how the village children were raised. And then the boys became pubescent brothers, and then husbands and then fathers—and you were to obey them all.

Even in her room in Dubai, after Teresa stepped out at five AM to attend to the toddler who woke up early, Huma would recite verses picked at random to compose herself. She imagined being back in her village hut with Little Mother and their spiny okra bushes and loofah gourd vines and, most fondly, their goofy chickens pecking the dirt.

At five minutes to six, Huma traversed the dew-laden grass to wash the pans that Nadir used to whip up breakfast for Mr. Suleiman who was headed to the bank where he was president, and for the five school-aged children Teresa corralled to the dining table, the toddler on her hip. The older children dared not fuss at Teresa in front of their father, the teen-aged twin girls completely silent over breakfast. They held their cheer, their tears, for their mother.

Madam would be down for her toast at noon, so she was no trouble in the mornings. Her energy perked up over the course of the afternoon and she came fully alive by eleven PM, when she either sent out for a recent Hollywood flick from the video store, nursing a splash of Jack Daniels from Mr. Suleiman's study, or a friend of hers pulled a Mercedes into the driveway. Huma liked the Jack evenings, as she thought of them, because Madam dismissed her once she was settled. The friend nights involved many preparations of mint tea and fried snacks that a bleary-eyed, sharp-tongued Nadir shoved at Huma to serve. Those were the only times that Huma resented Teresa, who always got to bed by eleven so she could come to the toddler at five.

But one evening, three friends of Madam's showed up at midnight. Huma was still in the kitchen wiping down the counters because Mr. Suleiman had been hosting a dinner for colleagues visiting from the London branch of his bank.

Madam had not bothered to greet his guests, all men. Teresa had instead been summoned by Mr. Suleiman to bring in their six-year-old son, Ali, whose facility with math he wished to show off. Teresa rushed back to the quarters and returned in the pencil skirt and georgette blouse she wore on her weekend outings with her friend who was a secretary at a travel agency, a friend Madam approved of because she knew the agency and the girl. Huma, bringing Teresa a cup of tea as she joined the company, noticed how her hair, freed of its butterfly clasp, glistened in waves. She regretted not letting Little Mother massage oil into her own hair more often.

The gentlemen, ensconced in buttery leather sofas, quizzed Ali in encouraging tones. The boy only shook his head and would not compute no matter how his father jokingly scowled. Finally, the child ran to Teresa, who had to set down her teacup in a hurry as the boy threw himself at her and hid his head in her lap. The company laughed admiringly at this tableau.

The men left after eleven and as Huma dried the last frying pan, she pictured Teresa back in their room untucking her blouse from her skirt, pulling on the silky white nightie that made Huma self-conscious about her own body with its flimsiness. The cook had taken off on his bicycle as soon as Mr. Suleiman's guests had been whisked off in a limo.

In the silence of the house, Huma heard Mr. Suleiman's study door shut and then lock. Surprised that he had not gone directly to his bedroom, she peeked out of the kitchen. He had looked tired from holding forth and bellowing jokes in an affected timbre all evening. Huma had even brought to him, unasked, a cool glass of lime water. He'd accepted it gratefully. Upstairs, Madam emerged from her bedroom made up with a light touch. She floated down the stairs trailing Opium—Huma had by now sniffed all her perfumes.

"Did his friends bring those English chocolates we love?" she asked.

Huma handed her a white and gold box that had been left on the coffee table. Madam smiled. "Nadir's shown you how to brew that cardamom coffee, right? My friends adore it."

Two of Madam's late-night visitors flew in the front door arm in arm, giddy as if they had just left a tip top party, followed by a third who did not bother to disguise the keen glances she threw up the marble stairs. As she tossed her abaya on top of the others on a brocade armchair, Mr. Suleiman burst out of his study. He tapped downstairs in his wingtips, glared at the woman, and exited through the gargantuan front door that had barely whispered shut on its pressurized controls. Huma saw all this and also heard Mr. Suleiman's study door shut again. Looking up, she saw Teresa scuttle from the study toward the toddler's room, still in her skirt and blouse instead of a work dress, pulling her hair roughly into a knot.

As Madam's friends made their way through two carafes of coffee and the whole box of chocolates, Huma washed and put away every pot Nadir had left sitting, swept the floor with care and even set out the breakfast plates and utensils. Brutish as Nadir could be, catty as Teresa was, she thought to ease the start of their collective day by giving them and herself a clean slate.

As Huma entered their room, she and Teresa exchanged a long glance. Teresa was already in bed, brushing her hair, the covers thrown off as if she were in a fever even though the AC hummed at the coldest setting. Teresa did not look away, as if daring her to ask a question. Huma blinked. She collected her night clothes and went to the bathroom to change.

When she returned, the room smelled of Dettol. The light had been turned off and the dim mermaid lamp between their beds, a reluctant discard from the twins because their father had disapproved of the exposed torso, threw speckled shadows around the room through its seashell shade. As Huma pulled up her quilt and her eyes adjusted to the light, she saw Teresa wipe a cotton ball beneath her collar bone and suck in her breath at the sting of the antiseptic.

Huma looked over. "Are you hurt?"

"He bites sometimes," Teresa muttered.

"Ali?" Huma sat up—the child was so gentle and so in thrall of his nanny.

Teresa turned off the lamp and faced away in her bed.

The AC revved up, drowning out even the silence between them. It was as if Madam had sent a signal with a reminder about not asking *who*. Huma turned to face the wall. She recalled a verse that she used to distract herself from an impulsive urge she knew not to indulge.

But in the morning, she awoke with Teresa's rustling and bolted up. The balm of the verses had evaporated overnight. The disquiet, a stubborn rash, was still upon her. "If that man treats you this way—if Madam lets him—why don't you leave?" Huma asked.

Teresa turned on the ceiling light that she usually left off so as not to disturb Huma. She smiled from her mirror as she tapped the Ponds onto her cheeks. "Can *you* leave?" Teresa retorted.

"I still have to pay back my recruiter. I have two and a half years to go on my contract." Despite the gold Little Mother had sold, they had had to borrow from the agent's agent. Besides this debt, Huma made sure to send Little Mother something every month to live on.

Teresa rolled her hair into a neat bun. "My contract expired six months ago."

"Then leave!"

"He has my passport just like he has yours, Nadir's, Fazal's."

When Huma had handed her passport over to Mr. Suleiman—the only time she'd stepped into his study—he'd slid it so casually into the top drawer of his desk that it had seemed as if she had handed it over for safekeeping. She'd thought nothing then of the key that had turned in that drawer. "And you haven't asked for it back?"

"He wouldn't give it. And now I've overstayed my visa. Do you know how much they fine you if you exit late? Where will I get four thousand dirhams?"

"So, what? You can never leave?"

"It's not so bad," Teresa mumbled through the bobby pins between her lips. "He's been paying me extra. Says he'll pay my exit fines whenever I do go."

"Then tell Madam."

Teresa laughed as she stepped out. "You think she depends on me only for the children?"

Sometimes, Huma thought, Teresa appeared to walk with Madam's gait. She followed her to the door to reconfirm her impression, to watch as Teresa stepped into the new dawn. When she opened the door she saw Fazal nearby, trimming the hibiscus hedge. He glanced up at her, then averted his gaze. She was still in her night clothes, her hair undone. She stepped back in, flustered. To her surprise, Fazal set down his clippers and approached her.

"What do you want?" she demanded in her sternest Urdu, steeling herself in the doorway.

He shook his head slowly and walked on to sit on the step to the cook's storeroom where a bottle of water awaited him. He took a long gulp.

Embarrassed about her suspicious reaction to the young man who was only busy with what he must do, like the rest of them, she modulated her tone. "Why're you working so early?"

"It's getting to be summer. The plants don't do well if they're trimmed in the sun."

"You like plants?" She hadn't met a man yet who paid loving attention to living things. Only boys who burnt donkeys with smoldering twigs for a laugh, men who dragged goats to slaughter.

He shrugged. "I'm responsible for them."

Huma found herself disappointed, more with herself than Fazal. She felt ridiculous for projecting a momentary romantic image on him. She was sure she had no thoughts about him. Though, once, he'd dropped a spade on his foot and sworn out loud in Urdu. The sounds of that swear had given her such a jolt of pleasure. She hadn't thought she'd miss the curses of the village boys, curses she herself yelled when Little Mother was not in earshot.

"How long have you worked here?" she asked him.

"Too long." Fazal poured some water into his hand and splashed his face. He leaned against the pantry door. It creaked open. Nadir must have forgotten to lock it. Fazal jumped up, yanked the door shut and grabbing his clippers, made for the bougainvillea on the far wall.

On her way to the bathroom, Huma couldn't resist jabbing at the pantry door. It gave. Perhaps feeding so many bankers had drained Nadir of his mindfulness, she thought delightedly. Or perhaps Nadir dangled his key from his belt simply to show off. A thought snaked into Huma's head. She knew she would not be able to kill it, no matter what verses she used to ward it off. She knew that she would have to find an opportunity to return and look around the pantry.

Though she had no idea when that might be, or what she expected to find, the prospect of an investigation, a discovery, imbued Huma with a preemptive boldness so that as she cleaned Madam's bedroom that afternoon, she found herself trying on one of her lipsticks. She had opened the makeup containers before, to look, to inhale the possibilities of, but never used anything. The lipstick was a lighter pink, one Madam used for her daytime looks. How could such little color change anything? And yet, Huma saw herself transform. She had never thought of her naked lips as dull before. But they glowed now, took on an aspect of health, of promise. She dared not open another container but wiped some lipstick off her mouth to slide over her cheeks. The highlights on her face brought a shine to her eyes. In that reflection, she felt new. She felt she had to know. And so, with Madam at the salon, the children not yet back from school, Teresa in the kitchen coaxing mashed rice on the toddler, she tried the door to the study.

The room was stark, more immense than she remembered, with dark wood cabinets up to the ceiling. The center was anchored by a solemn black leather sofa and two hefty chairs. Could that be where Teresa and...but no, the setting was too forbidding for irreverent imaginings. Her eyes wandered instead to the massive desk by the windows, devoid of all accoutrements—uncannily like the butcher's table back in the village, wiped down between cleavings.

She scanned the cabinets, their golden knobs like so many eyes staring back at her unblinkingly. What could they be holding? Forbidden books? Rifles? She wouldn't be surprised if Mr. Suleiman owned a sword or two, or at least a dagger. Now the drawers, those could hold cash. She'd even seen cash gathering dust in Madam's bathroom drawers—she never touched it. And what about the passports? A ray of afternoon sun glinted off the varnished desktop. Huma approached the other side of the desk and tugged at a drawer pull. It was locked as she'd expected. She looked for a wall clock to gauge how long she'd been there, who she might expect to run into if she stepped out. There was no clock here, though all the other rooms had one.

THE NEXT TIME MADAM VISITED THE SALON, she brought Huma with her. She was having henna applied for her niece's wedding and needed Huma's help while the henna dried on her hands. Madam introduced Shireen, the henna girl, to Huma. "She's Pakistani. I've known her for a long time. Maybe you can meet her on weekends. You never leave home."

"But—you won't need me?" Huma had assumed that Madam preferred she not take a day off, or at least, be summonable at all times.

"I might." Madam scrutinized the progress of the design lacing up her wrist. "But I worry sometimes that you may be getting restless."

Huma's heart dropped to her navel. Had Madam realized she had entered the study?

"And maybe she can show you where to buy some affordable makeup." Madam nodded toward the henna girl. "She would know all about that. She's been working here for years."

Shireen beamed, gave Huma her phone number scrawled on lined notebook paper.

Madam was thirsty, so Huma held steady a cup of diet Pepsi with a straw for her to sip from. Madam's hands and forearms, already bedecked, could not touch anything for several hours now. Huma tucked Madam's dress in as she settled into the car and opened and closed doors for her until she'd made it to her favorite chair in front of the TV. Huma used the remote to browse the channels until Madam spotted a film she might find tolerable.

The next day, as Huma cleaned Madam's room, she found the light pink lipstick in the trash can. She'd never taken anything, not even a dirham coin. But this looked like a resignation by Madam, like a sacrificed checkers piece. Huma chanted a short imploring verse as she lifted the lipstick, like she'd seen the old women chant as they attempted something prickly but pressing.

That night Huma was called in to help Madam dress for the wedding. She'd had her hair styled at the salon and needed help pulling on her gown without disturbing her hair. As Huma slipped the gown off its hangar, Madam slid her bathrobe off her shoulders. Huma froze. A long sunken scar crossed Madam's lower belly like a tight-lipped frown.

Madam laughed lightly at Huma's expression. "Some children are more trouble than others," she said, her voice gentle as if to protect Huma from her own pained imagination.

The form fitting gown required zipping up from the tail bone all the way to the neck. As Huma tugged the zipper while Madam sucked in her breath to flatten her belly, she tracked with her eyes a welt that arced from the middle of Madam's spine to what Huma had always thought of as the bone that her own wings might grow out of one day. This raised, jagged scar she had seen before: on the boys who had been whipped by the maulvi's switch; on Little Mother, who refused to speak about her many. Huma did not hesitate in her zipping, nor speed it up; she did not want to burden Madam with an unspoken question.

A jewelry box that looked like a miniature cupboard stood with its doors open on Madam's vanity. On its hooks dangled all the everyday earrings Huma had seen on Madam. From the last hook hung a simple two-pronged golden key. Madam slid out a hidden interior drawer of the jewelry box and chose from several dazzling options a pair of diamond teardrop earrings. Huma knew she would return to the room after the family had left for the wedding. Teresa was accompanying them to mind the younger children—she'd been fitted with one of Madam's evening gowns from before the kids. Nadir had been sent home early because nobody needed to be fed that evening. Fazal had no business there after sunset.

Huma ate at the time the family normally ate, rather than having to wait until their meal was done and she had cleared up after them. She fixed herself a plate Madam would have faulted as fattening and even popped open a Pepsi. She pulled up a movie on an Indian satellite channel. She sat in Madam's chair. She slid off Madam's chair. She sat on the rug close to the TV where she felt as if she were at the cinema. She lost herself in a Bollywood fairytale.

Bollywood movies are sumptuous and long. They leave you believing you can have more. Luck can be on your side. All you need is faith, and a fight in your gut. Teresa had said that these weddings lasted all night, that children fell asleep on conjoined chairs while the grownups danced. She got up to rinse her sticky fingers.

Madam's golden key in hand, Huma tried the study door. It was unlocked. Ashamed that the family had trusted her and she was acting in an unworthy manner, she told herself she would only look, and take nothing. The first lock she tried the key in was the top drawer of the desk. It was too large, too simple for that keyhole. She then tried it in this cabinet and that all along the wall. The key fit them all but wouldn't turn. She'd been avoiding the leather seating arrangement in the middle of the room but saw now that the long slim cabinet behind the sofa had locked sliding doors. She knew the key would work; she knew what the shelves would hold.

She dared not twist open any of the bottle caps lest she break a seal, but she could not resist a crystal decanter half full of amber liquid. The cube-shaped lid released with a gratifying clunk. She sniffed and scrunched her nose. Teresa's nail polish remover, she thought; honey; smoldering cow dung patties in Little Mother's stove. The stuff smelled worse than medicine. She wondered if Teresa had ever tried it—perhaps Mr. Suleiman had offered her some. She sniffed again. This opportunity would not return in Huma's lifetime. Unwholesome though its nature was, she could not resist its rarity. Huma whispered a protective verse, poured a splash in her palm and lapped it up. It was as noxious as she'd expected; still, a deep, warm sense of satisfaction coursed through her chest and belly. She liked the feeling of knowing.

As she crossed the sprinkler-wet lawn back to the quarters, she spied a dim sliver of light beneath the door of the padlocked enclosure that abutted their room. She wriggled the padlock. The only thing that gave was shards of rust onto her hands. She turned to the bathroom to rinse them. On her way, she poked the door to the pantry, as had become her absentminded habit. So far, it had always been locked. Perhaps Nadir had realized his mistake. But this time, the door creaked inward.

She acted fast to get ahead of the good sense she felt coming on, spoke aloud the verse of protection for a second time that day and pushed the door open. The pantry was dark, though she thought she heard a rustle. She did not know the layout of the room and stumbled between bulging sacks, steadying herself on drums, trying not to topple them. "Who's there?" she yelled.

This time the rustle emanated clearly from behind the wall of the padlocked room. Rats, she thought. She was not afraid of rats. But she did not want them in her food. As her eyes adjusted to the darkness, she saw between the sacks a narrow path toward the wall. She got down on her knees. She could have walked, but somehow crawling felt the most appropriate way to announce herself to a rat colony. She would mimic their posture, be a giant to them. As she got closer, she discerned a low crude door. She paused, wondering how many rats she risked encountering if she dared open it, then came up with the sensible idea that she should warn the creatures. She yelled the verse of protection for the third time and banged.

A growl and the door flew open. A creature larger than her leapt out, knocking her down. Man, it was a man. He smelled of grass. He seized her shoulders. Slammed her on the floor. She grabbed his face. "Fazal? Stop. Stop!"

He dragged her along the rat path, knocking down tubs. Then he dropped her and curled up against a far wall. She sat up, rubbing the back of her head.

She needed no electric light to see him, to see into him. "What have they done to you? Why are you not at home? Or wherever you sleep?"

"What home?"

"You sleep here? Nadir knows? Oh God, Nadir knows."

Still curled up, Fazal began to rock, his voice hollow. "He keeps me here."

"Nadir lets you stay here?" She knew she was staving off her own dawning understanding.

"He keeps me here," Fazal repeated. He would not look at her. "I lost my last job a long time ago. Mr. Suleiman watches over my passport in exchange for maintaining their garden. He pays me almost nothing. I can't afford a room."

"So, Nadir—he pays you by hiding you here? For…" She couldn't carry on; cursed herself inwardly for her cowardice, for yet again not asking directly; the way she had not asked Little Mother, not asked Teresa, not asked Madam. Instead, she opened an easier avenue—not one for a lie, but not one for the truth either. "What *is* that room?"

After a while, Fazal shrugged. "Storage. Papers in bank boxes marked in every language." He laughed a strange, truncated laugh. "Nadir's pulled together a few boxes marked in Urdu for me." When Huma couldn't stop staring at him, despite her decision not to ask, he looked as if he'd made up his own mind to speak. "It is convenient for everyone."

Since he had chosen to admit the truth, she would now ask Fazal the question she did ask Teresa. If she got the same answer from him that she had from Teresa, she would leave this house and this country and figure out another way to pay the agent's agent and keep a roof over Little Mother's head, or one day she, too, would turn into the haunted husks these two had become. But if he admitted he needed his humanity, she would help him.

"Do you want to leave?" she asked quietly.

To her surprise, Fazal's face wavered and dropped its mask. He burst into tears. She sat back quietly then, awaiting his next answer. She resisted a shocking urge to embrace him. She had never touched a man.

He wiped his nose with his sleeve. "But how? They'll jail me if I don't have the fine money."

Huma scooted up to him now. His cheeks were red, as if she had bloodied his face with her claws, his tears tracing violent streaks in the rusty flakes. She wiped his face with her own sleeve and sat back on the floor in front of him. "Why did you growl like that when you came out? Don't you know my voice?"

"Before you banged on the door, you were calling me the evil that Allah created, the evil of darkness. I thought you were going to attack me." His voice petered out as if he felt foolish.

"I thought I was praying for protection."

"That's only half the verse. You didn't know?"

Huma shook her head.

Fazal staggered up. "You'll call the devil down on you and yours one day," he scolded, more worried for her, it seemed, than angry.

Huma stood up too. One of the tubs that had tumbled had held a bit of olive oil. "Maybe," she said, her eyes on the puddle. The sound of *yours* echoed in her heart. She had never thought of anyone other than Little Mother as an extension of herself. Her father had abandoned them by the time she was four. When the echo would not recede, she bundled it away like a treasure to be explored later and said, "But now I'll bring my towel and bath soap and a bucket of water so we can clean this up."

The next time Madam settled in front of the TV, she called Huma over and handed her the key to the study cabinet. "You know where to find it, so bring me the decanter and a glass."

Huma found herself unable to budge.

Madam sighed. "Look, if he ever catches you crossing him, I will have nothing to say. You're lucky I was the one who smelled the spill in the study. Do you know how long it's been since I've scrubbed a carpet? Let this be the only time I have to clean up after you."

Huma brought her the decanter. So far, Madam had only ever come to the drawing room with a tumbler in hand. That night she made Huma sit by her and pour, and pour again. She said someone who really shouldn't have had told her she was beautiful. She watched *Top Gun*. She said she'd fought with her sister. She watched *Blue Velvet*. She said her head hurt. As the credits rolled on the second film, Madam sat there glassy-eyed. Without asking, Huma put an arm around her waist, coaxed her to stand, and helped her up the stairs.

It was three AM by the time Huma got into her own bed. The darkness reeked of Dettol.

At five, Huma bolted up to the sounds of Teresa's rustling. It was Friday, a half-day for everyone but her. She watched Teresa by the light of the mermaid lamp as she dropped her nightie and picked up her daytime dress. A raw slash seared across the flesh of Teresa's upper thigh. She would not meet Huma's eye. Huma felt the throbbing of the welt as if it were on her own body. She had seen the bitterness a lifetime of silence had engendered in Little Mother.

She followed Teresa to the door and watched. Teresa did not waver on her daily course. Fazal was not yet by the hibiscus or the bougainvillea. Nadir would be in the kitchen within the next half hour. He might need something from the pantry soon. Huma stepped out in her night clothes and tried the pantry door. It was unlocked. She slid in and crawled down the rat alley. At the door to the hideout she whispered, "Can you find me a small screwdriver and a hammer?"

A scrabbling and then, "Look in your bathroom after the men leave for the Friday prayers."

"And you—look under the sack by this door before the sundown prayers."

"Huma?" Fazal called, and then paused as if considering. "What is your full name?"

What did it matter in this hour, on this day? Still, she decided to give voice, in that room of confessions, to a thing she had known for a while but not yet dared speak—a refutation of the fact, the lie on her government papers. "I've disowned my father."

Fazal cleared his throat, stalling, as if he were processing her words. "Huma Bibi, then."

Huma knew that, on Fridays at sundown, Teresa went to see her travel agent friend. But that was later. First, the driver would take Madam, Teresa, and the children to Madam's sister's for lunch, and then return to pick up Mr. Suleiman, Nadir, and Fazal to head to Friday prayers at the mosque.

On other Fridays Huma took a welcome afternoon nap before everyone returned from prayers and lunch and the needs of the household resumed. That day, she stood in front of Teresa's mirror and looked at herself for a long time. The screwdriver and hammer waited on her headboard. She combed her hair and then, not trusting herself with verses anymore, applied a layer of the lipstick she had stashed in her suitcase. She saw again the shine it had brought to her eyes and smiled in the mirror. Keys were only one way.

In the quiet of the house, she tried the study door, took a deep breath, and entered the room. Going around the desk, she inserted the screwdriver into the lock of the top drawer and hammered it in gently as far as it would go. She wiggled it at every angle. She jiggled and hammered and knocked and twisted. It gave.

Inside, amidst leaky pens and dirty coins from every country of the world, lay five passports. She recognized her own right away, as well as Fazal's. She had to flip through the others, and shoved Nadir's and the driver's back into the drawer. Quickly, she checked the lower drawers, all of which had now been unlocked as well, but found only red ink pads and rubber stamps. The passports by themselves would not be much help.

She thought of Madam's closet, where she knew she kept her various purses but first she would try Mr. Suleiman's room that was separate but connected to Madam's via their bathroom. In the top drawer of his dresser, he kept his accessories. She lifted the lid of a black box that she'd always assumed housed his many watches. But it was full of cash—a deep stack of five-hundred and one-thousand-dirham bills, with the pale rubber bands she recognized from when he handed them their salaries. She was relieved not to have to take anything from Madam.

On the way back to her room, she tried the door to the pantry. It was locked. She kept her calm. In her room, she tucked her own and Teresa's passports and part of the money into her purse, then slid Fazal's passport, the rest of the cash and the tools under her pillow.

After that she called Shireen and asked if she might visit that evening.

Soon, the house was abustle again. Nadir rushed to and from the pantry in preparation for dinner. When he lumbered out with a particularly heavy load, she snuck in. She placed Fazal's passport and seven thousand dirhams under the sack by the little door.

When Teresa returned from the villa to get dressed for her evening out, Huma followed her to the room. She, too, changed out of her work clothes. As Teresa picked up her purse, Huma grabbed hers as well. "I'm going out today, too."

Teresa raised an eyebrow but said nothing.

They walked out of the villa's heavy front door together, letting it hiss to a close behind them. As they waited on the porch for the driver to pull up the car, Fazal wheeled Nadir's bicycle to the garden gate.

He appeared to be in a hurry. He looked back only to say, "Khuda hafiz, Huma Bibi. We'll meet again!"

"Bibi?" Teresa asked.

Huma shrugged. "Just a respectful term for a lady."

"Nadir's going to mind about his bicycle," Teresa said, leaning against the portico pillar.

Huma shifted from foot to foot. She had to finish what she'd started before the driver arrived. They were not likely to have another moment alone. She grabbed Teresa's hand and placed on it her passport with five thousand dirhams tucked inside.

Teresa tightened her hand around the little bulging book. She looked down and fingered it gently as if it were the face of a long-lost child.

"Go," Huma whispered. "Your friend is a travel agent, no? She can help you."

Teresa's grasp relaxed. She slid the money out, counted it and sighed. "And what do you think I have to go back to?" She straightened the bills and tucked the stack neatly into the back flap of the book. "My auntie's shack?"

As the car pulled into the driveway, Teresa held up a finger to sign to the driver to wait. She took a ballpoint from her purse, eased out one of the thousand-dirham bills, and wrote on it a phone number. "This is my friend Lina—at the travel agency." She handed Huma the bill. "She's

Lebanese, so she speaks Arabic. She can get things done, if you can convince her."

Then Teresa heaved open the door to reenter the house. Huma followed her but could not bring herself to let the door close behind her. One foot in, and one out, she watched Teresa take the steps up to Madam's bedroom and enter without knocking, as easily as if it were her own.

Top Nanny, Season 5

Houston, 2019

When Yara, our long-time babysitter, qualified for Season 5 of Webflix's hit reality show *Top Nanny*, she texted me right away. As I read her note out over dinner, Mo and the kids cheered. Our laptops, phone chargers, and composition books sat jumbled on one end of the dining table. We'd pushed them aside to make room for kababs still in their two-day-old Styrofoam take-out containers, the onions gone limp and sulfurous. Neither Mo nor I had traveled for work the week of Yara's auditions, so we could split school and club drop offs. The kids missed Yara's grilled cheese sandwiches and complained about the visible bits of green chilies in the kababs, which, I'll admit I'd ordered medium instead of mild because when else would I get a chance to train them on spicy food?

The real marvel came with Yara's follow up text. *BTW, Noreen?! It's going to be your kids with me on the show, right?? Like it just has to be!!!*

The kids yelled, "Please, please, please?"

Of course, Mo and I said yes. Yes, Yara could be paired with our kids for Season 5. After all, she'd shepherded Amad through his first lost tooth, and now Tina through her first period. More importantly (though we'd never say this out loud because we like to keep our kids grounded), wasn't this how stars were made? Mo and I didn't end up in this neighborhood in this city in this country by ignoring open doors; once our feet were in, what were a few crushed toes? Sure, Yara would be the contestant. But it took just a couple of episodes of Season 1 for viewers to realize that it was the kids who made the nannies.

Take Marina from Season 1—the twelve-year-old, not the nanny. (About Marina-the-nanny, what could they have been thinking letting her on the show without a driver's license, so she had to tow her toddler around on public transportation? Is it any wonder she lost the child at a farmer's market in the very first episode?) Marina-the-kid set the definitive bar for charges with her finely tuned sense for when to let her nanny shine and when to bring her to tears. If you ask me, all that off-screen tabloid drama, with the kid's teenaged sister being hospitalized with an eating disorder in her failed attempts to outshine her little sister on the show, is not the producers' fault. What fourteen-year-old needs a nanny? Back in Pakistan, she'd *be* the nanny.

Marina-the-kid was such a hit, viewers flooded social media with demands that she return in Season 2. The producers caved. I told Mo it would be impossible to replicate her exact chemistry with a new nanny. And I was right. The kid ended up in a rivalry with her own nanny, and the pair got voted out after a catfight at the spa birthday party episode. The fact is, though, that the girl now has one hundred thousand followers on TikTok. She does astute cringe-inducing skits about girl-on-girl jealousy. They say most of her followers are moms.

Now Mo and I would never coach our kids, but we've spoken privately about how Marina's trajectory might be an advisable strategy for our own Tina. The season won't start filming for another two months, and she's aging out of the show with every hour.

The night of Yara's acceptance, Mo and I let the kids take their phones to bed so they wouldn't show up in our room on a rare weeknight together. Over a bottle of pinot, we convinced ourselves that our little one, Amad, had the potential to last through Season 8. The record so far is two seasons. Everyone said Khloe, who won Season 3 and 4 with that French nanny, had another season in her. But, my friends, burnout is real.

Not for our Amad though, who's kept up with his soccer club despite a repeat broken ankle and two concussions, all of them from post-game disagreements with his teammates.

Honestly, Khloe, too, was a strategic error on the producers' part. They should have picked either her piano plus ice-skating or her competitive dance for the nanny to handle, not all three—TV isn't real life. The nanny went on late night shows afterwards, promoting her new parenting book, touting how, unlike over here, French kids take naps after school and play outdoors until dinner. (Mo snorted and reminded me that's what we did in Pakistan too, but who'd buy a book about that?) By the way, Khloe is more than fine. With a little therapy after Season 4 (thank goodness for open-minded parenting in this country), she already has her own clothing line for pre-teens with her signature duck-lips logo. Imagine if Amad had his own logo on sneakers. (Though, he'd better come up with something savvier than the rainbows he's been drawing since he was five.)

The kids don't know that when Yara agreed to stay on with them after her first year—unlike their prior nannies—we bumped up her pay by fifty percent, and have done so again every six months since then. Soon, she dropped all her other part-time jobs, and then even gave up college (which I was against, but Mo told me to get over my desi mindset already). This last year, she managed to afford both a personal trainer and a stylist for her *Top Nanny* auditions. Of course, she got in! If we hadn't done this for them, how would Tina and Amad ever have gotten their shot at TV?

Now it's up to them. We can't be there episode to episode, raising Yara's pay every time they connive against her. Our babies are going to have to make it to the finish line on their own. We'll be cheering them on as they grace our home theater screen, determinedly hands-off like the French parents in that book. Given the decades of media consulting experience between us, perhaps Mo and I do know a thing or two about upping show ratings, but the kids need never find out.

Mailee and the Saint of Horses

Deorhi by Lahore, 1950

The kumhars of Pakistan, they have a book. It is called *The Potters' Book* and you might yet uncover a crumbling manuscript in the Storyteller's Bazaar in Peshawar if you ferret out the current whereabouts of Haji Fazal & Haji Abdur Raheem & Sons, Booksellers. This tract would affirm to you that Hazrat Adam, the first man, was also the first potter. He wielded tools brought by the archangel Jibril by the command of Allah. You would learn that the prophets Nuh, then Ibrahim, then Ishaq, then Musa, and then Muhammad—peace be upon them all—carried on Adam's work and entrusted it to the kumhars through seven hundred patron saints of the profession.

But most precious to the potters among you would be the tutelary verses for the Digging of the Clay, the Kneading of the Clay, the Setting of the Pots in the Kiln, the Opening of the Kiln, and every step of your craft in between. Your wares would be blessed if you could chance upon this guidance.

There is one copy, however, that you will not find. It is dust now, buried with me, the blind saint who stole it from his own father, the master potter, the ustad of the kumhars of Deorhi.

As a child, I spied my father struggling to decipher the parchment by the glow of his kiln, crackling those stained, translucent pages sown to cardboard, the cover gnawed away by worms. I knew my father could read none of it—he could not read at all. The man only knew the places and the sounds of the few verses taught to him by the ustad before him.

And I—not yet blind—attempted to make sense of that script while the other kumhar boys treaded the week's ration of raw clay with their feet. It's not that I had no affinity for clay. Has not each one of us—me, my father, your father, you—come from clay? But it was the utilitarian nature of the ustad's passion that I had failed to inherit. My father accused me of an obsession with the useless; my father who turned out pieces intended to last generations—faithful cooking pots, trusty water urns, hardy planters; my father who turned out women's things.

So I thought to impress the ustad in my own way—by coming to know what he only pretended understanding of. I feigned religious fervor so that he begrudgingly handed me over to the mosque's maulvi to whom I said, *Teach me to read, not just recite.*

But once I had mastered the nuances of diacritics, begun to perceive possibilities where the maulvi saw commandments, I could not return to the mosque, nor to my father's workshop. Instead, I returned to clay and lost myself in molding and firing horse after horse. Have you seen a horse not yet broken? Then you have seen a spirit as pure, as potent as the angels cast from light.

And though my playthings exasperated the elders, the boys back from the clay pits with their loaded donkeys would gather around me at sunset to listen to the yarns I spun at a miniature carnival of horses until their mothers chased them home with canes.

"Can you not see, Israr, that you're destined to be the next ustad?" my father demanded to know as I gathered my horses in the lap of my tunic.

My unearned fortune did not move me to industry. So, I was cut off from the task of creation. I was relegated to fueling the kiln with cow dung.

And I—not yet a saint—was first followed by a girl whose name no one could remember; it had vanished with the death of her mother. They called her *mailee,* "dirty one." But when I called her Mailee, she told me by the washing stones at the river, from my lips it sounded like "one from the dirt."

She liked dirt and the shapes it could take. I'd stood at the entrance to her father's workshop and watched her entranced by the sodden lumps that danced on her father's wheel and took life in his fingers while she ground black stones for her paint. And before her father had even reached for his wet cotton thread to cut away a new pot, she seemed to know what vine would trail around its girth, and what flowers would bloom on this vine, and no two pieces she painted were ever alike because she knew their spirits.

I, who used to loiter in every workshop but my own father's, was taken by the soul in Mailee's painting, and one day, my head in a rush, I led her behind my father's workshop and, lifting a water pitcher from his towers of wares, showed her how to trace on to it verses from *The Potters' Book*. As I guided Mailee's brush hand with my own, we were caught by my mother.

You know what my mother said. Her words came from the same place as my father's pottery. She would not have her son taken by a filthy motherless girl, even if the girl's father was a kumhar.

She dragged me by the collar and threw me in front of my father's wheel. She flung the pitcher that Mailee and I had been so intent upon at my father's feet. It exploded against the wheel with a thunder that released my mother's tongue from decades of shackles. She assailed her husband for raising a son who would dilute their blood into so much slip.

Consumed by her own rant, she did not notice me writhing on the floor from the pain of shards in my eyes. The ustad must not have perceived my agony either, nor did he hearken the rest of his wife's tirade when he discerned on a fragment of the shattered pot a recurring part of the blessing for the Opening of the Kiln.

He lifted the broken piece to his lap. "Where did you learn this, Israr?" His words were gruff, but not harsh. His voice wavered between a sense of pride that I knew the sacred verse, and a pang of jealousy that someone had partaken in the revered knowledge that was his to guard until he chose to pass it on. He had never thought I cared for *The Potters' Book* and its lessons.

"Tell me where you learnt this, boy!" he repeated more urgently.

I replied only with a howl, my fists to my eyes.

They washed my eyes for many days, but my sight first blazed red, then smoldered down to darkness and after forty days, I never saw again. I could not read anymore, and the other boys had little time to visit with me. From the window of my room, I heard them conjecture that I had been punished for making idols.

But Mailee, she came every day. My mother allowed this, surely guilty for having been instrumental in my plight. Outwardly, she proclaimed that it was Mailee who was the cause of my ruin, and so it should be Mailee who cared for my needs.

Under Mailee's vigil, I healed. And, during this time, she begged me to teach her how to mold horses from clay—so I did, for my fingers could still see as well as ever. When we tired of horses, we adorned the walls of my room with verses from *The Potters' Book* in raised clay, at that time a bottomless source for me to draw on because we wrote at the stumbling pace of dirt. We slowed down ethereal time with the friction of the material, and that is how I kept from tumbling off the edges of my knowing. Tell Mailee, if you see her, that this was all I knew.

This, and her. Mailee, I grew up by the kiln. Mailee, I could not go back to the flame. Fire was my blood. It ran through my veins. Mailee, I was taken from it before I knew what to make of it, what to make from it. And I was left with grit in my eyes and a handful of words like stars in the night of my head. Stars are not news. But we make stories of them, as many stories as there have come eyes into this world. Mailee, you spun tales with me. If you see Mailee, tell her she restored me by taking my coarse horses to her father's kiln and bringing me back finished dreams.

I received her gifts but would not—could not—touch her hands. I guided her only with my gestures and my words. I had held her hands once and lost my sight, my way in the world, and couldn't yet imagine how I would find another path. You think I had none of my father in me? I had his jealousy, a streak so vulgar that it wrapped a noose around my own: though Mailee and I had been together that day, she, unlike me, was unscathed.

In the time it took for my ache to abate, an agony that was the long, emaciated shadow of my physical pain, my mother had another child. I sensed my parents' grief lighten and confided to Mailee my relief that at least they now saw another future.

I did not tell stories to my little brother, relinquishing his mind entirely to the ustad. But it was not long before my brother skipped home reciting absurd, lowly rhymes he had picked up in the alleys, and our father brought him to my room.

"Teach him the verses from our book so he can make Deorhi known for its kumhars in far flung lands." The ustad's voice was plaintive.

I sensed a surrender, an offering of peace, an acknowledgement. But the harshness of a learned truth is hard to temper; the arrogance of youth, harder still. "Don't you know, father," I said to him, "have you never understood that those verses are for all craftsmen? That our people have simply recast them in the words of potters?" Emboldened by the silence of my father, the breath I heard him suck in, I offered, "I will teach my brother the entire truth of these words so they can sustain him in any path he may choose. But I will not put those verses through your potters' sieve so that all he is left with is the stingy gravel of your world."

"Heresy!" The ustad's voice shook. "You change the book to suit your purpose."

"How do you know?" I said this turning toward my brother so that neither my father nor the little one would know who was being addressed.

It was then that the ustad proclaimed that I was banished from his house and the clan. Banished. He would listen no more. Not to my brother. Not to my mother. I was banished.

I asked for one more night during which I prepared to leave. Among other acts of cleansing, I sanded down the walls of my room. And after that I did not go far. At the outskirts of the village, I built myself a hut of mud strengthened with straw that Mailee gathered for me. Around the hut I raised a low wall on which I placed clay horses of every aspect. I scraped the feet of each horse, then scraped the ledge of the wall so the horses would be joined to the wall by the sun so firmly that not even the monsoon winds could rend them off.

The folk of Deorhi, and even those from villages nearby who knew how I had insulted the ustad, avoided my dwelling. But one stormy day a despondent man arrived in the hopes of an apprenticeship with the kumhars. Drenched, he knocked on door after door. Mailee, emerging from her father's hut, knew that the kumhars barely had the heart to feed their own, and led him to take shelter with me. There, she and I heard the drifter's tale.

"Show him," Mailee said to me. "Like you used to show the other boys."

It had been so long since I had paid heed to another's story. So long since another's question had worried at the sediment in my mind. I told the man a parable of my own creation, one that was a mirror to his story. The man heard. He got up. He said he saw. He forgot about the lessons he had come to seek from the kumhars and asked me what he could do for me in return. I asked only for a horse in payment.

"A horse?" The man cried that he was too poor.

"A clay horse will suffice," I told him, and relieved, he left.

I then scratched the story I had told into the wall of my hut. This hollowing, this removal, was faster than the making Mailee and I had done with our raised script in my childhood room. This time, I did not worry that I would run out of material in my soul, because I had found a way to create again. But to make a record of it, I had to contend again with the limits of my physical world, the very substance of my shelter.

Mailee ran her fingers in the grooves I made. She said she wanted to keep up, made me teach her to read my new tale. But I would not let her practice by copying it into my walls. Those walls were all I had. And with every mark I made, I took from their integrity. Maybe you've heard that Mailee memorized my tales instead.

Maybe you've found somewhere in the world her brushwork. Tell Mailee, if you see her, that I've forgiven her for giving you my stories. Perhaps she thought I had wanted you to have them. That you might find something of your own in them. Did you think I had nothing of my father in me? Laugh then, when I admit that I had mulishly intended each story only for its first listener.

The first man Mailee had brought to me was grateful and when he next returned, he brought not only a clay horse but also three other drifters. Under Mailee's urging, I began to summon stories with the frequency of others' needs. It was as if her insistence were the breath from a bellows, rekindling my will until I did not need the inspiration of a supplicant. Even before the sun had risen and launched another traveler on the road to my door, I began to cast new tales and Mailee would come to read them before a stranger might lay eyes on them.

When the people arrived, she showed them to the sanctuary of the Saint of Horses.

"What is your sorrow?" I asked each one.

I began to send forth more creations into the world than did the workshops of the kumhars, my works guarded in their hearts and not dangling from sticks in cloth bundles.

The ustad watched all of this with trepidation. Since business trudged along, the ustad told the potters, "Never mind. Keep your hand to the wheel and the true word will help us prevail. His tales are just the dazzle of a traitor's mirage."

My visitors began to bring with them mica and tinsel and I let them hang it all up because they said it gave them the comfort of other saints' shrines they were familiar with. I knew that beneath the adornments, my walls were layered with my own work.

The glint of the strangers' ornamentation seemed to deride Mailee. "Why do you do this to your room?"

I knew she meant the garish decoration. "It is the scaffold for my next story," I answered, waving instead at the web of my scrapings, illegible by now as they bled into each other.

She would not give up—even when she realized I did not need her anymore. Tell Mailee if you see her that need is not the same as want.

When visitors began to come from so far that they did not know to bring a clay horse with them, she began to grind down the discarded mistakes of other potters and fire her own clay horses. She gave them away at my doorstep so no visitor would be turned away without an audience with the Saint.

With her practiced hand, she began to fashion horses more elaborate than any seen before so that in the mind of the people, she became one with me. Tell me, do you not include her in your legend of the Saint of Horses? In those days, she suffered for this confusion: she, like me, was also written off by the clan as lost, aimless. Mailee, what did they know? They had not lingered on your creations as I had, tracing every rise and every fall on those forms soaking in the warmth of my hands.

Mailee began to paint her horses. I could not see the patterns myself, but my visitors were so enthralled by the pieces that they hesitated to part from them and only did so after describing to me in detail the ornament on their offering. They stayed longer and asked me to read into the painted horses for them, layering her thought with my own stories and braiding new meaning for themselves beyond what I had intended. Mailee, for her part, never interpreted her patterns for them. She stood on my threshold and thrilled in hearing them described, in watching me strive to articulate her lines.

Then one day, she enshrined a horse in a webbing from a paste mixed from her own kajal. This one she brought to me herself. I received it from her hand, listened to her describe what I held.

"And what is your sorrow, Mailee?" I asked. Still, I did not take her hand.

She left in shattered silence.

I heard that she marched to the ustad's house and shouted, "Where is your book, ustad? Can it teach me what I need to know, because I have not found the answer in all these years?"

I heard that the ustad, who would normally have ignored her, was disturbed by the relentlessness in her voice and stood up from his wheel to go in search of his long untouched volume. He had not brought it to the gatherings of the kumhars after the night of his final words to me. It would have been like ripping off the scab that protected his heart.

He led Mailee into the courtyard of his home, asked her to wait and ducked into his bedroom. The neighbors heard such a crashing and a slamming that they rushed out to see. The ustad hurtled out of his compound, his hair wild.

"Lost!" he informed the world, tearing at his kameez. Then he screamed at the sky, "The word is gone!" They said the crows in the courtyard took wing, their caws echoing the ustad's wail.

That day, Mailee walked away without the word but with a new understanding. She must have seen that I had left my father's house with a piece of him. But I had not settled with the man. She must have realized this—that this was my sorrow.

After that, the ustad's kiln never turned out pitchers that could hold water and the kumhars of the village saw no more customers because it became known that their pottery had no soul, as if it was not blessed. Much of this was said by the continuing stream of visitors I received. The ustad died from a wasted heart.

I was not prepared for this. I had been meaning to meet him in his workshop, a man now, to speak with another man.

Mailee, she guessed this. As the gravediggers prepared the earth to receive his body, they hit upon a clay of a hardness not seen before in our area. They tired of their labors and had to break for the sundown prayer before continuing their work. The ustad's final tragedy—that he had not been buried before sundown on the day of his death. In the descending dusk Mailee crawled in the brush to the unfinished grave, knowing full well the injunction against women in graveyards. She grasped a pointed rock that lay in her path and brought it into the grave with her. Lowering herself into the dank hole, she scraped out the unyielding clay, hiding a lump in her bosom as she was discovered by the keeper of the graveyard.

The village had tolerated her ways thus far, but this desecration was too much to bear. In their general sorrow they did not even ask for an explanation before sentencing her to twenty lashes. In the days that she healed, she kneaded the lump until her fingers were calloused, but it finally gave and she molded it into a small horse. Once the totem was fired, she knew it needed no adornment.

"Israr?" she called from my threshold. She walked in without waiting for me to acknowledge her.

I had no need to ask her why she had brought me another offering. I had heard the talk from the village, so I received the horse from her hands in silence, knowing it before I even held it. I opened the trapdoor underneath my pillow and lowered the horse into the opening.

With my fingers, I traced the welts that had broken open her back. I cupped her hands in mine. I reminded her how two pieces of clay must both be scarred before they can be joined. That was also when I dared ask her name again. She had said by the washing stones that she would never tell me because she liked my rendition of "Mailee."

"Mashal," she answered.

You've heard how our son, Kalim, was trained by Mashal in his father's art. I had watched her for years, and so I taught our son something of his mother as well—that as long as he knew his own name, he would never be lost.

She did not verse him in his grandfather's book. He was but five when she had him lower *The Potters' Book* into my grave along with the horse that had stood upon it beneath the trapdoor.

Little Mother

Deorhi by Lahore, 1973

As you rip out with your bare hands the stalks in the heart of a sugarcane field and screech from the sting of a thousand translucent thorns raked up by your palms, as you disembowel the dank earth in search of a bone severed from your sister's spirit that would not be broken, as you stomp the clumps of sod with the inhuman strength your muscles have sucked out of your now hollow heart, you fail to hear the footsteps of the village maulvi.

He has emerged from his mosque, beard and kameez whipped by the winds, a hand on his cap and three older boys from his madrassah flanking him; he has come because your otherworldly wails had been sullying his call to the sundown prayer. Your feral eyes give him pause; he has to avert his gaze from your heaving chest with no dupatta to shield it, from the way your muddy white shalwar clings to your calves. He overcomes his reluctance to touch a woman not his wife—perhaps you are not a woman to him right then, perhaps a thing barely human—and drags you by the wrist to your widowed mother's hut. He flings you at her feet and demands to know what she means to do about you. You lunge at him so that he scurries out of the door, holding it shut to keep you in.

The village elders have gathered, the women tell your mother the next day; they have agreed with the maulvi that you must have disturbed a djinn's resting place and it has now possessed you, become one with you, made you delirious. The women squat on your mother's dirt floor. They are not afraid of you, the way the maulvi had been, because they have seen this madness before, perhaps lived it themselves. They rock lightly in rhythm with your mother who rocks you as you lean in her arms, the salt burn of your tears still on your cheeks. They do not meet your mother's eyes because she has only just lost her older daughter and now must confront a possession of the younger. As the winds pick up outside, their thoughts turn to their own hearths and they concur with the elders that for the djinn to relinquish you, it must be beaten out of you by a man of God. Your mother leads you to your cot, then snatches her broom and brandishes it like a sword at the women. As they hasten out, she locks you up inside the hut to keep them from you, and you from them.

If she ventures out for water or flour, the women admonish her that her obstinacy is selfish, that the djinn will begin to take root in you. In the alleys, the maulvi's students stone her with insults and are not chastised. The butcher cheats her and is not fined. The elders threaten to convene about her obstruction. At home, you are still a terror. She tires. She concedes.

And so, on the night of a new moon, they lay you face up on your stripped cot and tie your hands to the wooden posts above your head and your feet to the ones below. As you grab the knobs of the bedposts to brace yourself, your finger finds the bite marks you had made in the wood when you were a cheated child and too small to fight your sister for the rest of your jaggery lump. Your lips crack into a dry smile at the memory of that day, for all you have left of her are memories, while they—they peel away your clothing until your mother tears off her own shawl to cover you. At the dreadful sight of your smile, they touch their ears with their hands and whisper prayers of absolution.

The maulvi strolls in swishing his cane and commences to menace the djinn. He chants verses that he taught you himself many years ago in a one-room school at the back of the mosque, through a curtain. Out of habit, you almost recite along; but the whistle of the cane agitates you, reminds you of the time this same stick had flogged your sister for giggling in school. You remain silent, your breath stifled.

As the maulvi's chants fall into a rhythm, the others recede, dragging your mother along. The bolt clangs from the outside. After that, at the foot of the bed, the holy man removes his crocheted skullcap, steps to the right side (for he is still left-handed after all these years of repentance), swings the stick in the air until its whine arrives at his preferred pitch, and sets upon the djinn by striking the soles of your feet; lightly, at first.

They say that such beatings hurt only the djinn and not the possessed one.

Soon, you don't know which is louder—your own cries or your mother's hammering laments at the door. Amidst the din, they will not know that the maulvi has set aside his cane and needs no implement to assault the djinn that he says is deep inside you. Meanwhile, they assure your mother that your howls are not your own, but the protestations of the djinn.

"When all is silence," one of them scolds, "the djinn will have departed. Let the maulvi do his work."

"Quiet down, Kausar," your mother yells. "Silence, my child."

So you moisten your parched tongue with the sweat that has trailed to your mouth and summon one last time the strength you did not know was still in your heart that is so spent. You hush your djinn.

By your silence, you compel the holy man to shorten his work on you. It appears that the djinn may have left much sooner than the maulvi had expected, and he is obliged to reign in his own heaving grunts. He lets out a curse that only a man with much accumulated divine forgiveness dare squander. He retreats after a parting lash that your mother has to salve for a week before you can sit again.

Afterwards, they counsel your mother to keep you indoors to give your ravaged body time to heal from the assaults of the djinn. You slink along the walls of the house, from the stove to the window to the cots to the stove, always quiet, to keep your djinn calm so they do not suspect him anymore. You cool your flesh against the mud of the walls that carry a dampness from the rains that have not abated since the maulvi left. Nobody comes to ask after you because they are chasing after their roofs that have been shorn away by the storms, rescuing their bleating goats from sudden streams that rush past their doors. The first morning you wake without an ache, the rains give way to a mist.

When the new moon next cuts a sliver in the sky and you have not bled, you know that something has taken root in you. Your djinn has taken on a new form. You are delighted. You are anguished. Your mother—what will she tell the others?

And so, when the message arrives from the village Chaudhry's mansion that his son, Faizan—Chhote Sahib they call him—is ready for a new wife, and that he will have none other than the beautiful younger sister of his beautiful first wife, you nudge your mother and whisper your acquiescence to her.

But even though the Chaudhry owns much of the land in the village, as will his son after him, your mother is deaf to you. "I cannot," she tells the matchmaker. "I will not."

The matchmaker is unfazed and appeals to your mother's pride. "Listen Naziran Bibi," she says, "the truth is that the Chaudhry is shaking in his jootis right now. Imagine the insult upon him if his son is refused by a possessed girl."

"Tell his son to give me back my first girl before he asks for my second one."

"Don't you know, sister? None of his peers will give their daughters to Chhote Sahib. They know all, even if they do not speak. The Chaudhry dares not even approach them."

Your sister had birthed Faizan but one daughter, a ferocious little imp of a girl, Huma, and that only in the fifth year of their marriage. You alone knew that your sister still pined for her second cousin to whom she had been betrothed since childhood, but who had to be turned away by your mother, powerless as a widow to refuse a proposal that arrived from the Chaudhry's house. Faizan had seen your sister at the tube well bathing with her cousins, the girls unaware of being watched at a time when the men should have been in the fields. He claimed he had been bewitched by her laugh.

One day, in a fateful moment of nostalgic passion, your sister escaped her husband's home to meet her old love at the guava tree of their childhood. There, she was spied by the Chaudhry's farm hands.

That night her three-year-old daughter, playing in a corner of her parents' bedchamber, tripped over her mother's severed braid still entwined with her mirrored ribbons. It had been sliced off cleanly, to shame her. At sunrise, the same farm hands who had observed the tryst by the guava tree discovered most of the rest of your sister pieced into a gunnysack caught in some reeds downstream from the village. They never found her head.

They do say that Chhote Sahib and his two best friends were seen lugging another sack into the sugarcane fields on the night the braid was found. No one dared check what the men left in the sugarcane, not because the people feared a severed head but because the Chaudhry had announced with finality that it was nothing.

Your mother had not believed the Chaudhry, but she could not say that aloud, even to you. Nor could you say anything to her. But you had gone to unearth your sister's head when the maulvi found you.

Every passing day, your little djinn has bloomed as much in your heart as he has in your abdomen, and so you squeeze your mother's arm to reassure her.

"No, Kausar," is all she says back.

Your djinn will not survive without the name of a father in this world. You convince her with a new whisper: "Huma needs me."

Huma is all that walks upon this earth of her first daughter. She relents.

Two weeks later, the Chaudhry's household arrives at your home with a palanquin. This palanquin is more handsomely carved than the usual village ones, elegant with curtains of pink silk. Your mother seats you in it with her own hands and she cries all the more because it is the same one she had given away her first daughter in. You are carried off to the Chaudhry's mansion by the groom's cousins and his two best friends of the sugarcane fields. No one has bothered to look inside since the last wedding; musty brown marigold petals swish about and crumble underneath as you settle in.

You place your henna-laced hands on your belly into which your djinn has descended. He does not flutter yet as he will many months hence but reposes, suckling on your insides. You are woken from your reverie by tiny footsteps pattering alongside your carriage. You reach up, bangles jangling, to crack aside a curtain and peek.

It is Huma. She catches your eye and addresses you as "Little Mother" on this morning of your wedding. You will miss being her khala but decide that this way she and you can be closer. Someone has rouged her cheeks but her hair is matted and uncombed so that she reminds you of your discarded doll. Every now and then, she catches up with the palanquin and leaps up to swipe her finger along the swirls etched into the poles weighing on the shoulders of the men.

The other children are daring each other to peer into the window. None step forward. In the heat of the game, one boy insinuates that the bride is in fact a witch disguised in red garb whose curse would land upon the first person to see her face. Other children declare the curse to have the power to bring grave harm to the mother of the cursed. At this, Huma screams with burning cheeks that her new mother is no witch.

To prove it, she jogs up to the window and yanks aside the curtain. "Little Mother, look at me!"

You shift your veil and take in this child, now almost five. She has been kept from you since your madness and you have ached for her. When you smile at her, she returns your smile shyly and falls back.

At the Chaudhry's home, you are brought to your bridal chamber and seated on an ample poster bed graced with satin and rose petals. It is the same room in which you had helped birth your sister's daughter, whom the Chaudhry's wife now leads into the room.

"Greet your Little Mother, child," she orders as she presents Huma to you.

"Salaam, Little Mother," the girl obeys. She knows, and you know, the redundancy of this exchange and a silent smile passes between you. You lift your veil and reach for her hand. She lets you take it. Your new husband strides into the room then, so you let the veil drop. His mother caresses his head, wishes him a life a hundred years long, and seven sons to carry on his lineage. As she leaves, she yells out to a servant girl to hurry in with a cup of warm milk for the groom who will need his strength.

Faizan indicates the door to Huma with a flick of his finger. "Hish!" he says to her.

When she does not budge, he stomps his foot as if at an unwelcome kitten. The child spins and darts out of the room. He follows and shuts the lumbering wooden door behind her.

As your eyes track him from under the veil, you notice between the bases of the two curtained windows of the room a small arched cutout fitted with amber glass. Through the bubble-clogged glass of the cutout peer two little eyes. You lift your veil once more and shake your head at the child, careful not to jingle the jewels pinned to your hair. When she does not move, you purse your lips in a begging kiss and nod her off. The eyes disappear as the bolt latches in place.

Faizan approaches and proceeds to unburden you of your bangles one at a time. Your mind wanders to the quandary that you have not thought of what to call him. You decide to address him simply as aap—the formal "you" will suffice because he is not likely to have a need for you to address him by name. His breath is quickening with each bangle so that when he has removed them all, he is unable to focus on your earrings or nose ring but instead lays you back, reaches below the hem of your wedding skirt and rolls it up. You turn your head to the side and catch once more the eyes in the arched hollow. Your eyes lock with hers as he takes you.

Many nights pass in which he takes you and you see her shadow outside the cutout you have blocked with a chair, and many days pass in which he is gone to the city on the business of the farm and you oil and comb her hair and feed her parathas and rich curries with your hands.

At the next new moon, your djinn tells you that he should be made known, so you vomit out your breakfast in front of the Chaudhry's wife. She sends tidings of the good news far and wide.

Four moons later, when Huma lays her hand on your belly, she says that the thing kicks as if it were impatient. Another two moons after that, your abdomen sears and throbs with its engorged prize. The Chaudhry's wife frets that such an early baby will be too frail and sends for the maulvi to come and chant verses of protection.

He comes with his skullcap and his loincloth but not his stick this time. He lowers his gaze in your presence since you are after all the Chhote Sahib's wife. Closing his eyes, he begins to recite, and lo, your darling comes alive as if he recognizes the verses of his origin.

"Raise your eyes to me, Maulvi Sahib," you say as you pull aside your shawl and reveal your undulating belly.

He glances at your face. When you force his gaze to your womb, he falls pallid; he bolts from your bedchamber. He has to veer around Faizan who has rushed in, having received the news that your time was near. Your husband raises his hands as if to hold you. But he has never before brought his hands to you except in the dark of the night, so he is unsure and drops them again. Just then, the creature pushes as if it would grow as large as your entire self and burst out of your skin. Your shudder is so immense that a dread comes upon your husband and he, too, retreats from the bedchamber.

You release a howl and break into the sweat that will last until your djinn is finally out of you. The room has been full of them, the midwife, the Chaudhry's wife, the cleaner and God knows who else. The only eyes you look for are the ones at the arched window, eyes that you hold through the last push as if they were a hand in your hand.

When they place the babe in your arms, your labored breathing gives way to a laughter so terrible your husband will not reenter the chamber and the Chaudhry's wife and the midwife and the sweeper scramble out with their fingers in their ears. They had accused you of harboring a djinn and so you did. The infant gazes at you with lucid eyes wide open, from a face too intelligent for having just emerged from a cocoon. Laiq, you decide, you will name him Laiq.

Alone finally, you crawl off your bed towards the window, your newborn in your arms. You tear off the curtains to let the sun set him aglow. He glistens with your inner life that they did not scrub off before escaping. He does not like the light of the world, having been gestated by your darkness. He wails, his lithe limbs reach, not like damp new butterfly wings, but like a bird ready for flight.

At the glass arch, Huma's eyes are wide. You beckon her in. She disappears and a second later, races into the room.

They say that when Chhote Sahib saw the girl scuttle for the doorway, he shook off his trance and chased in after her, as if not wishing to allow her to approach his son first. (For they had told him by then that he had a boy, and a mighty fine one for having been two months early.)

When they enter, you are slumped against the wall, the writhing thing ready to leap out of your arms. You have to clutch him to your bosom and hang your sweat-drenched locks over his face to block out the light to calm him.

The man and the girl reach you at the same moment, his stride overtaking her darts. He makes as if to pick her up by the scruff of the neck when you yell, "Leave her!"

He staggers from the slap of your words. He has not been chastised for two decades, and never by a woman.

The girl is still as a stone idol, her eyes flicking from you to the thing in your arms and back to you.

"Come," you say to her.

"What are you doing?" the man demands, but his voice has a tremble. "My son will not be touched by the child of a whore."

"Huma is your child too," you tell him.

"I cannot know that." He spits out those words and oh, how ridiculous his petulant visage is.

You cannot repress the cruel inside you, the truth. "You are right. You cannot know. Neither about your daughter. Nor about your son."

"What do you speak of woman?" His mouth trembles as if he had been stripped naked in the village square.

"Come," you say again to Huma, your voice calmer for the girl, your warning eyes still on him.

She approaches you as you hold the man pinned with your glare. When she is close, you tuck back your hair and reveal the infant to her. She stares at him, her curiosity and fear of her father in a tug of war.

"Make a circle with your arms," you say.

You place him in her waiting cradle. "Do you know what a djinn is?" you ask.

She shakes her head.

"A being cast from fire," you say. Eyes still on Faizan, you tell her, "This one is ours."

"Yes, Little Mother." She snuggles her offering.

Faizan turns and exits the chamber. From the threshold, he accuses you of relations with a djinn. He leaves for the city for many years. On farm business, they say. His mother diverts her attention to the marriage of her next son, and the old Chaudhry takes to his bed.

The patriarch refuses to allow a divorce in the family. His son refuses to enter the home while you still haunt it.

Your mother, out of hope for you, builds up the courage, the defiance, to visit the widow Mailee Ma, some local potter's ostracized daughter who lives with her son on the periphery of the village, revered by forsaken outsiders for her wisdom, and, some whisper, black magic. Mailee Ma counsels her to bring you home.

You visit your mother, and they send no one after you.

They will say afterwards that together, you, your little girl and your little djinn had no need to keep count of the moons. You bide another kind of time.

A Shade for the Window

The woman materialized one bitter winter morning under the graf-fitied awning of the vacant taqueria. The shop had sat boarded up since its last tenant clattered away in a pickup truck ahead of a rumbling hurricane. Though slight in aspect, she wielded a rake as if it were nothing but a sisal broom. Haroon noticed her as he maneuvered his bicycle to his bus stop across six bustling lanes of Hillcroft Road.

Leaning his bicycle against the bus shelter, Haroon regarded the way the new woman's powder blue shawl draped on her head, flowed over her shoulder, was tucked just so behind one ear—she had to be Pakistani. She purged the sidewalk of a muddle of plastic bags and organic refuse as if the act marked the place as hers. Haroon had never seen an occupant of this stretch of road pay heed to the street front, all peevishly ensconced in their lodgings and businesses as if what or who dwelled outside did not matter, as if they themselves could not matter outside those walls. Houston was a city of interiors.

Haroon missed his grandfather's leafy verandah in Lahore, the child-hood games he'd played there with cousins and neighbors. He even missed the baked-sand playgrounds of Dubai where he had found escape in soccer for the few years his parents tried to make a living there. He often gave a disengaged new student in his class the benefit of the doubt because he remembered the wilds of American schooling he'd been released into as a lonely fifteen-year-old, ignorant about deodorant and mediocre at English. He'd picked up the English, some fashions as well, but the jokes, two decades later, still gave him trouble.

Perhaps the new woman struggled with English too. Even here, she wore her shawl as if a disapproving brother might appear around the corner any moment and chide her for lapsing in her modesty. She gathered the trash by the chipped tile counter beneath the awning. The late taqueria, converted from a shawarma stand, converted from a juice and tea shack, converted from an immigration, insurance, and tax office, stood in a two-story property that broke up a chain link of carnicerías on one side and halal meat stores on the other. No one expected the termite-gnawed structure to stand for long, let alone afford a living. No one knew who owned it, or why the developers of the adjacent strip lots clawed their way around it. Its sign board, painted and repainted, had faded and peeled so the names of its occupants merged indistinguishably. Over that counter Haroon had bought tacos—not halal—many a night after his mother had gone to bed, and before that, when the shop was a shawarma stand, he'd brought home shawarmas—halal—to his mother as a Friday evening treat.

He was on his way to the high school where he taught math. As on every morning, he had ducked under the gate of his apartment complex, careful not to brush flaking paint and rust with his gelled hair, and raised his hand in farewell to his widowed mother. She watched him from their window, a squat obelisk, her white dupatta still swathed around her head from her dawn prayers. She waited for him silently all day, the only non-Spanish speaker in the complex; then unleashed her pent-up Urdu on him when he returned.

The screech of a braking bus startled him. The woman, who'd glanced up at him several times, squinted and adjusted her shawl with an air of finality, as if to dismiss his gaze—a gesture he'd seen his cousins back home make in markets when strange men stared at them.

On the bus ride to school, he thought the woman, given her demeanor, might be in her forties. Over lunch in the teachers' break room, he recalled the shine on her cheek, striking even from a distance, and imagined her a decade younger, closer to his own age. By the time he unlocked his bicycle in the afternoon, her face had resolved into a fine-featured blur of the starlets on the Hindi film posters in the desi grocer's windows, and he worried she might be barely twenty. That was the problem with women. Their attitude and their apparent age could not be counted upon to reflect each other.

On his return, as Haroon lifted his bike off the bus rack, he saw the abandoned building aglow with new life. Its tattered awning had been removed. Light from the setting sun danced off the shop's scrubbed aluminum shutters. The woman's shawl was aflutter in the window of the second story. Two shadows crossed the blue curtain back and forth. A teenaged girl emerged at the casement. Her eyes wandered down and connected with Haroon's. He waved, but she shrank back under the curtain. Self-conscious of his own awkward interest, he pivoted toward home. But sensing another movement from the window, he glanced up again. The older woman now peered out at him from behind the shawl. She held his eyes and didn't look away as he expected. The surprise put such steam into his legs, he cycled away, breaking up their wordless exchange.

As he tucked his bicycle under the stairs, the comforting smell of toasted flour from the rotis on his mother's griddle wafted down the stairwell. He stepped in to the sound of the slap of dough between her hands.

"Any news, Ammi?" His usual greeting, offered without pause as he passed the kitchen on his way to wash up before dinner. He did not run the water as soon as he reached the bathroom, curious for once to hear if she had anything to share.

"All by the grace of Allah, son." Her usual response summarizing the monotony of her day. He turned the tap to full gush. He wished she would visit with their acquaintances, Fazal, the halal shop owner, at least, and his wife Huma—both of whom they'd known back in Dubai and who lived nearby. His mother's niece, Noreen, lived further away, in the inner loop, which was too far to get to without a car. Besides, his mother had had some falling out with the young woman when she lived with them in Dubai. She did call Noreen's sister Shireen though. Shireen owned a salon in Dubai now, a salon Haroon remembered her working at. The last owner of the salon had been exited from Dubai, his mother had told him with relish. Levied with a big fine for committing employment fraud. Some rich patrons set Shireen up to take over instead. Tired stories of the past. Fantasies and fabrications, even, he suspected. That was all his mother talked of. She did not trust new connections.

Returning to the living room, which doubled as his bedroom, he dropped to his bed and tore into the rotis laid out alongside a bowl of thick lentils. From his mother's bedroom he heard a shuffle different from the sound of her preparations for the sundown prayer.

She emerged shaking out a white cotton sheet. At one intersection of folds, the fabric had stiffened from age and crumbled. She clucked at it. "Never mind." She brushed away the detritus. "It will do."

"For what?" He tried to modulate his tone, maintain brevity so as not to express too obvious an interest. His mother could neither abide being ignored nor being upstaged.

"After you've eaten—and don't hurry your meal—go give this to the new woman across the road."

"But why?" The sheet reminded him of those used to cover the floor at his father's funeral prayers.

"Just like your father. You men always need a reason." She groaned as she lowered herself into the only chair in the room. Its wicker frame creaked out a threat to snap another string from its woven seat. "Is nothing I need important?"

"Ammi, please." Exhaustion settled in the nape of his neck.

"She's hanging the shawl off her head for a curtain. Who knows where she came from? In what circumstances? A single mother, showing up like that—in a shop, not even a home." She sighed, her brow pained.

"The second story has living space—"

"Tch tch…" His mother dismissed his rationalizing. "She has a daughter with her. We should do what little we can to protect the honor of a young Pakistani woman."

She told him of how, when she had ventured out to the grocer's that morning, she had overheard the construction workers' mothers gossip about how no one had seen the new woman's man yet. They guessed the woman was a cleaner sent by the secretive owner who was finally prepared to sell the building. They wondered about why she kept that shawl draped over her head. "If I could speak their tongue, I'd explain to them she's Muslim."

Even after two decades in these parts of Houston, she hesitated to converse with "Mexicans"—her designation for all non-desi brown people—in anything but her plodding British-accented English. If she struck up a friendship with some of their neighbors, he often thought, she wouldn't be so dependent on his company.

He rose from his meal to rinse his hands. Catching himself in the mirror, he reached for his comb. Back in the living room, he picked up his mother's gift. "I'll be back."

AT THE SHOP, uncomfortable with the intimacy of the side door that led to the rooms above, Haroon knocked on the shutter at the counter. After a second knock, a stream of light flooded from the window above. The shawl had been pulled down.

The woman emerged from the side door, the shawl hastily flung over her head. "It's you."

She'd addressed him in the familiar form in Urdu. Her cadence mellifluous, even in such few words, did not have the quarrel of his mother, nor the wile of the grocer's wife or the Bollywood-inspired flirtatiousness of the grocer's daughters. Hers was the voice he imagined of the narrator of the Urdu fairytales he used to read as a child. Where had those books gone now? He couldn't remember having read anything but English in years.

She had guessed he spoke Urdu as well.

"Yes." He smiled to acknowledge her friendly tone, surprising himself. Flustered, unable to think what to say next, he gestured admiringly at the clean shutters. He wasn't sure if he meant to compliment her work or ask her about her plans.

"Thank you. My coffee stand would be open tomorrow if I had some beans and milk," the woman answered both his thoughts. She had understood.

"Ah, a coffee shop." That was all he could muster. He was speaking to a woman. But he spoke to women all day—his colleagues at the school, so many others he had business with. He remembered his business and handed the woman the white sheet with a brief explanation.

"Please, thank your mother for her kindness." She was as calm as he had been abrupt.

He had a question. How to ask it in Urdu without sounding too forward, now she'd chosen to use the familiar address between them? He fretted for the first time that he'd lost his finer sense for the language, speaking it for years only with his mother as a son, and, since his father's passing, as a provider.

"What name can I give my mother?" He'd managed not to say "you" or "your." He wished she'd volunteered it herself.

"Shama." She laughed. "And what name can I give my daughter when she asks who brought us this gift?"

A joke. He hadn't volunteered his name either. He smiled, found himself shielding behind English. "Haroon. I teach. At Percy High. Math."

She nodded, then continued in Urdu. "We don't have much. Some clothes and dishes, a coffee machine for our shop, and... some sugar."

How strange, yet entirely fitting, that she would have nothing but sugar. He wanted to ask her more, hear her speak more. But he had no more messages from his mother.

"You should open your coffee shop in the morning anyway." He turned away before she could ask what he meant because he wasn't sure either.

IN THE MORNING, at the sound of his clanging about the kitchen, his mother called out from her bedroom. "What are you doing? I just finished my prayers. I was going to make your breakfast." She stationed herself in the kitchen doorway. "Why the hurry today?"

"I'm leaving now." He brushed past her, a mug of milk and a sandwich bag of ground coffee in hand, ignoring her cries of *Allah, what has gotten into this boy today?*

His heart raced from having been so abrupt with his mother. His supplies balanced in one hand, he grasped his bicycle under his free arm. At the edge of Hillcroft he paused as delivery trucks and speeding commuters honked past each other. He looked over at the coffee shop, expecting the shutters to roll open any moment. There was no way he could cross his daily divide with this new burden.

His eyes roved his side of the road for options. The grocer, lazy pig of a man, never unlocked his doors before eleven. Haroon told himself that if he left his bicycle resting against the shop door, passersby might assume it belonged to the grocer.

Across the street, the upstairs window was now shaded by his mother's white sheet, as if she had already blessed the dwelling in her own manner. It had been done out of kindness, out of concern. And yet, and yet. No gift was ever truly free. It was as if she had raced ahead of him, changing the course before he was even upon it.

He stood in front of the shop and considered how to announce himself. The shutter clattered open. Shama and her girl stood looking at him.

The girl smiled from behind her mother. She resembled her mother but had the wiriness of youth shedding adolescence. He hesitated to smile back because he'd seen the kids at school grin that way when they thought they knew more than the person they hid behind. The girl shrugged and receded to the back of the shop to pick up a book.

He set the milk and coffee down.

Shama picked them up. "Will you have some coffee?"

"Yes. Yes, thank you. I didn't have time for coffee at home this morning."

He glanced back to check on his bicycle. It had slipped to the sidewalk, forcing people to walk around it onto the street.

At a nod from her mother, the girl ran upstairs. She returned shortly with as many clean mugs as she could cradle.

Shama twisted open her jar of sugar, nestled inside which sat several cinnamon sticks. As she started the coffee, Haroon told her about his school in the city. He complained about some tiresome students who did everything but the work he assigned them—all things he had planned to tell her as he tossed in bed the night before. In Urdu, he'd promised himself. If he did not talk about himself, he would have to ask her why she had come here, alone, barehanded. He did not want to know who she had been, because his mother was right, there was nothing good Shama could possibly say. If he kept telling her about himself, she'd keep asking more in that voice of hers.

When Shama turned to attend to the coffee, he checked on his bike. The girl caught him looking that way and came forward to peek as well.

Shama poured some of her brew into a tall mug, sprinkled some sugar, swirled in milk and handed it to him.

He inhaled the faint scent of cinnamon that lingered in the steam. "Won't you join me?"

Shama splashed some coffee into a mug, handed it to the girl, and poured a bit for herself. The girl stole away with her coffee, as if afraid it might be taken back.

Shama set her own mug down on the counter, untouched. "Zoya's father died last year."

The girl didn't bother to look up from her book. She recrossed her legs nonchalantly as if that statement, the story to follow, was stale to her. Haroon set his mug down too. How to keep sipping during such a revelation?

Shama glanced once at her daughter and then continued, "His family says I'm cursed because he turned frail from the day I arrived as his bride in this country. His mother had wanted to keep me with her back in Lahore while he worked here. They had expected my youth would guarantee them an heir, a grandson around the house to light up their final years." The girl kept her eyes averted. "Now they won't allow a cursed woman to return to the bosom of the family. Not even her daughter."

How was it that she could bring herself to tell him all this? How did she know he would not shun her like others from the community might, others had? She was taking a chance. He nodded. "And your family?"

"They're still back in our village. My mother won't accept the shame of a daughter unwelcome in her marital home. They'd given me away when I was as old as this one. How can they take me back now with a girl as old as the one they'd married off?"

Zoya looked up. "And so, *you* have no home." She spoke in that way teenagers have, of telling ungracious cutting truths.

Shama closed her eyes as if drawing on her reserves of patience. "A home is where you make it." She did not turn around but raised her voice for the benefit of her daughter.

Haroon wondered about the girl's accusatory tone. He thought it unfair toward Shama. Perhaps Zoya had imbibed her grandparents' rhetoric. Children were sponges. How alone Shama must feel. "What will you do?"

"My parents' neighbor's uncle has owned this building for a long time." She described how Mr. Zakir had moved back to Lahore in his retirement because his family in Houston claimed they couldn't afford his healthcare. He was angry with them and refused to sell his only property or bequeath it to them. Somehow, her father convinced Mr. Zakir she could take care of it, though her mother was opposed to the shame of her living here by herself.

"But your husband's family won't have you, and your mother won't have you, so where does she imagine you could live?"

"Such questions are irrelevant for mothers, where moral matters are concerned."

He couldn't argue with the truth of that.

"So, here, I'll earn something and send my girl back to high school. She's missed so much already."

Haroon felt grateful for Shama's trust, a heady urge to convince her she could rely on him. Not in the way his mother relied on him, as was her right and his duty. But in the way two people who owed each other nothing might.

"Zoya," he ventured, "Would you like me to bring you some books to catch up?"

The girl looked up at him, and then behind him. "Wasn't that your bike?"

He turned to see what she meant by the past tense. A teen in sagging pants was wheeling away on his bike.

"Oy!" He raced to cross the road despite the traffic. The boy whipped his head back to look and lost his baseball cap. Haroon picked it up. He was about to throw it at the receding bike when he caught himself falling to the level of the thief. He tossed the cap into the scrub by the grocer's shop and trudged back to Shama.

Zoya had come up to the front to watch the proceedings. "Sucks," she said, expressionless.

He shrugged, accepting her commiseration.

Shama smacked her daughter's shoulder. "What language at a time like this!"

Zoya spun around, grabbed her book and left.

Haroon wished he could defend the girl on this technicality, even though he'd felt little sympathy from her earlier, perhaps even derision. But he didn't know how to explain "sucks" in its entirety in Urdu.

"It's alright," he managed.

"How will you get to work now?" Shama looked around the shop as if she might have something lying around that could be of assistance; as if she was used to hunting for possibilities even in a void.

Absurd. And he had been foolish. He raked his fingers through his hair for a while, then looked up across the road and considered his own street. "I have to go."

As he stepped away, he paused and turned back.

This woman was causing him to go against his own survival instincts. First, he'd abandoned his bike, and now he was returning to say goodbye. Stopping to take leave never got him anything except instructions from his mother and requests for inconvenient favors from acquaintances. He had learned not to explain himself. "I'll ask the guys in the complex for a ride into town on one of their pickups," he told Shama. "Probably look for a new bike. But if I do, I'll have to get something for my mother too. She does not like to be forgotten."

THAT EVENING, THE UNFAMILIAR SIGHT of a cab pulling up to the apartments brought the small children out to ogle. As Haroon hauled a recliner up to the apartment, he ignored his mother's refrains of *What was the need?*

Moments later, his mother, glowing in the bliss of her new chair, did not object to his also having spent a few dollars on books for the new girl. In fact, she sent one of the boys from downstairs to fetch Zoya to come get them. Something in the air loosened her tongue; she attempted broken Spanish to instruct the boy.

Shama came with her daughter, so Haroon's mother offered her tea and fed Zoya a ghee-laden paratha. "The child needs some meat on her bones." Shama was subjected to a piqued glance.

When Shama said she wished Zoya had a tutor, Haroon's mother asked what good her son was if he couldn't do this small favor for them.

Haroon hesitated, worried about dealing with the girl's contrary attitude, but his mother glared at him. He relented, having learned by now the futility of challenging his mother's judgments of him founded on her own imagination of his intentions.

So, it came to be that he visited the coffee shop several times a week without his mother demanding any explanations from Allah. Instead, she sent along hot chicken curry for Zoya, and once, at the Eid festival, even handed him a silk for the girl from her own storage chest. Shama made acquaintance with the grocer's wife and, through the woman's community connections, acquired some spare furniture, including a worktable for the coffee shop, at the end of which Haroon tutored Zoya in math.

After her lessons, Zoya preferred to take her assignments upstairs and Haroon and Shama waited in the coffee shop for her to return with her completed exercises. The two talked mostly of their childhood, both interrupted by a removal to this country.

"How grownup I'd felt at fifteen," Shama admitted to him one day. "So ready to make a life with a man I'd never met. I know better now."

Haroon felt his ears flush. Here was an opening, perhaps an invitation, to speak a thought he hadn't fully formed for himself. He blurted out, "Did he come to love you?" He'd been coaching himself not to filter his thoughts with Shama, the way he had done his whole life with others. It was impossible, for one, to say directly to his mother what he meant without offending her—she needed to hear things her way.

"He never told me." Her eyes were far away.

"But did he, at least, show you care?"

"Perhaps." She got up and gathered their mugs. "I was too young to realize I needed more than gestures." When he looked jarred, she laughed and sat down again, her fingers still entwined in the mug handles. "I can see that your mother cares for me and Zoya."

"Gestures don't come from nothing," he argued, surprising himself. He was trying to make sense of this unmet need she talked of. This dismissal of a form of expression, a communal understanding of intention.

"But a word carries commitment. This is why we choose it with care when speak it aloud to God and to the courts—"

Zoya came downstairs with her finished exercises.

"And to each other," Shama finished. She left the two of them to work through their equations.

Haroon found himself relieved for the moment. He was on even ground again, talking the reliable language of algebra. But he was determined not give up on his Urdu with Shama. His time with her transported him to a world that was comfortingly familiar, yet enticingly unexplored. She, too, kept watch for him, seemed to set aside her other cares to talk of things she had spoken to no one about for decades.

His mother would send for Zoya every Sunday to feed the child, she said, her only real meal of the week. The grandmother of the boy who was dispatched to fetch Zoya began to visit with Haroon's mother while he was at work.

The women found that hand signals interjected with Spanglish and Urdu were adequate language for camaraderie between neighbors. Sometimes, Haroon came home to the sound of laughter that rang of conspiracy between his mother and her visitor. There was an anticipation in the air the women tamped down when they became aware of his presence, readjusting in their seats as he walked by.

One evening, after his mother's visitor had scurried off just before he returned from the washroom, Haroon asked what had caused them to become such good friends all of a sudden.

"Hope." His mother flashed a smile of mutual understanding at him.

Never had a word from her sparked such a twinge of joy in his heart. "Ammi, we need to talk." He sat down to his meal, finding himself hungrier than usual.

"What is there to say, son?" She poured more milk into his glass. "Of course, I approve. I've been waiting for this day for years, and just when I had lost hope in this forsaken land, Allah delivered a daughter to me of his own accord. Now all I need to be at peace is some money for the wedding preparations."

"But shouldn't someone at least talk to her?" He was taken aback at his mother's assumption of acquiescence on Shama's part.

"Women understand, my son." She chuckled. "Never mind, never mind. I'll set your heart at ease and go over tomorrow to talk over what is already understood."

"But Ammi, there are things that should be discussed, things you cannot say for me." He pushed his plate aside. "I'll talk to her myself."

"What could you possibly need to talk to her about that we women cannot resolve?" His mother sat upright, petulant again in a way she had not been since the new chair.

Where could he begin? If they ever had a lengthy discussion, it was rarely on any matter other than subsistence.

"Our home situation, for one." He got up. "We'd need room for four."

"My dear boy!" His mother eyed his unfinished meal. "What need would Shama have to move in with us when she has her shop to run? You and your wife can have my room."

He set down his glass of milk with care, afraid it might spill along with hasty words that would not serve his purpose. She should not be made to feel opposed. He was all she had. She knew that.

"You don't trust your mother, I see." She picked up the Quran that sat on her side table. Her eyebrows took on the pious aspect she reserved for special moments of supplication in prayer. "As God is my witness, I'll treat your wife well, and she will not need another mother."

He strode to the window and scanned the street. Cars rushed past, their headlights mocking him as if he were doomed to stand still forever. He could not bring himself to turn around, look at his mother's face. He could think of no other way to tell her. "I want to marry Shama, not the girl."

He heard his mother struggle out of her chair and limp off to her room.

He followed her and halted in her doorway. She lay on her bed with her face to the wall, a scarf tight around her head—the way she lay whenever her head pounded with a pain caused by the only child born of her womb.

"Ammi, listen."

"You would bring a cursed woman into this house," she moaned at the wall.

He steeled himself for more lines from her favorite Urdu soap operas. "She's only a widow," he tried. "Like you."

"Which is why she should know better and take pity on me. She did away with her first husband. And now she would enter my home and take away my only blessing. Woe be to the day I let her over the threshold of my house…"

He determined to cancel their satellite TV subscription on the pretext of expense. "She has never, Ammi, never intimated to me any desire of marriage."

His mother sat up. "Don't make it worse, son! Allah protect my ears from such abomination. Do you mean to tell me she consorts with you without considering marriage? Abuela warned me about her. I see now why they allow their own sons and husbands only one coffee a day at her shop, no matter how special they claim it is. Cinnamon," she huffed. "Who knows what else sits in her sugar."

"You don't understand." He was struggling. "I would never marry that poor child. Don't you see? She's too young."

"Too young for what?" His mother donned a confused expression. "Abuela says she might even have introduced to us her own granddaughter, who is the same age as Zoya, if you didn't have the problem of not being Mexican."

"They're Nicaraguan! And why do you call her *Abuela*? She's not your grandmother!"

"So? She calls me Ammi. Am I her mother?"

"You've all lost your minds!" He turned away from her door, sickened, afraid of encountering "Abuela" if he stepped outside.

"I'm not saying anything needs to happen right away, son." She followed him out. "Can't I wait a bit more, when I've waited so long already?" Her voice turned conciliatory. "In any case, we may have to save for a year or two, to have enough for the wedding."

When he didn't respond, she snapped, "Don't underestimate me the way your father used to."

Haroon was tempted to pick her up by the shoulders and shake her. The shock of that impetus propelled him out of the apartment.

"Haroon!" His mother called after him. She sounded distraught, in true anxiety for herself. "What will Abuela say?"

He could think of only one person he'd ever felt the urgent desire to converse with. He traversed his street, found himself at the closed shutters of the shop, went around to the side door, banged on it with his fist.

WHEN SHAMA FOUND HIM at her doorstep, she saw his state and led him upstairs. She had to know how inviting him into her living quarters must look. But she didn't hesitate, so he didn't either.

Her stairwell was dark, damp. Haroon was glad to emerge into a lamplit living room at the top. Pulling the door to the bedroom shut, Shama offered him a seat on a small plaid couch. Save for a round rug the chair rested on, the room was so vast in its emptiness he was afraid anything he said would echo off its bare walls. He wondered if she knew the chair was called a loveseat. He could not take it because of the irony of it. And if he did, then where would she sit? It wouldn't be appropriate for them to sit so close together given all the proper distance the rest of the room afforded. Whatever his mother imagined about Shama, they had never gone past conversation. He knew her by now—she would only do the appropriate thing, not as much to set an example for her daughter as to hold herself to her own morality.

And the more he had wanted her these months, the more he had wanted to wait for her. She was an enigma he did not want to resolve for two moments of present pleasure. She was, to him, the misplaced past he wanted for his future.

When he would not take the seat, she sat down first. With a wave toward the other side, she invited him to join her. He sat instead on the rug by her knees and could barely muster the strength not to take her hands uninvited. Of all the things he wished to tell her in those moments, he found he had waited too long and dared only to begin with his mother's stated wish.

Shama listened, her face still, a flash in her eye. "And will you not tell me what you wish?"

If only he could describe to her all that he dreamt, then pull a switch like a rail operator, split his track from his mother's, carry Shama away from the shadow of the accusations she had come here to transcend, to never look back. If only. "I told her Zoya is like a daughter to me."

Shama searched his face, waiting for more.

His chest tightened from disappointment in himself. He had shifted the burden of their mutual admission, their next turn, to her. Of course, she gleaned this was not the entirety of his argument with his mother, the entirety of his confession to her. They remained silent for so long, Shama got up.

He had expected he'd leave if he could say no more, but he found himself surprised by her leaving. He moved to the chair and reached for her hand to guide her back to the seat. To his relief, she let him. Her hand stayed in his.

Letting out a deep breath, he braced himself. "I told Ammi it is you I want to marry."

She gave him a wry smile. Slid her hand free. "You once asked me my name so you could tell your mother."

"Have I said something wrong?"

"You've said nothing yet, so how could it be wrong?"

He tried straightforward, unembellished words in his head. But they seemed inadequate, plebian, crass even, right out of his mother's soap operas. How was it possible that the sublime being he imagined a lifetime with could be satisfied with such artlessness? He searched for what to say.

She would not, she told him then, live a second lifetime of waiting, of gestures.

When Haroon returned home, he followed the steps past his apartment door as if in a trance, broke out on to the bare flat roof of the building and fell asleep under the open sky. When the sun rose so high the cement beneath him was warm, he awoke. He tumbled downstairs past his apartment. On the ground floor, his new bicycle waited for him. If he stepped out, his mother might be looking anxiously from her window, her white prayer dupatta tucked around her head. She had never spent a night alone.

He tiptoed back up and cracked the door to the apartment. She wasn't at the window. Perhaps she'd taken to her chair to pray on her tasbih beads for his safe return. Most likely, she'd taken to bed, her scarf knotted around her aching head.

He stepped in to the clicking of her gas lighter at the stove.

"I cooked your favorite sooji halwa after my fajr prayers." She did not turn to check on his state. "Go wash up. I even made dough for pooris—they'll be all fried up by the time you're ready."

Halwa poori—each bite a nutty-sweet creaminess enveloped in rich flaky pastry—the meal of communal celebrations. His mother had had some news, and she was satisfied. He slammed the apartment door behind him and ran past his bicycle, under the gate, down the street and to the edge of Hillcroft. It was so late, even the grocer had begun to rustle inside his shop.

The grocer poked his head out of his side door, a reeking garbage bag in hand. Spotting Haroon, he snorted. "Why are you not at school today, teacher?" Without waiting for an answer, he lobbed the bag into a dumpster and slammed his door shut.

Haroon took in the closed shutters of the coffee shop. Upstairs, the dark window gaped. A ripped plastic bag fluttered by the counter and caught on the bar of the missing awning.

I Breathed You First

I breathed you first—
—even though he claimed you.

That drenched winter morning you were still new to our town, Iram. You crossed my mist-laden window, all kohl-lined eyes and plum lips. I thought I was the one falling, but then you slipped in the mud. I ran out barefoot, more to see the creature you were than to check if you were unhurt.

Your head in my lap, you would not blink; those unflinching pools reflected the rainbow of me, gave me vertigo. My lips to your ear, I whispered *It's okay. You're okay.* I thought to say, *I'm here,* but just then my broad-shouldered brother strode out of the house and towered over us, legs splayed. You fluttered your eyelashes, languid, beseeching. He had no choice but to rescue you. In one swoop he lifted you into his arms and said, *I'm here.*

And me? You ruined me by leaving your fingers laced in mine a moment longer than was necessary.

He spirited you away and laid you on the divan in the drawing room. Dirt-streaked, I followed, then stopped in the doorway as he tucked a raven curl back from your temple. Mother was summoned. Her older son's marriage prospects, despite our family standing, had begun to look bleak. She had given up on improving Abid's manners. Instead, she'd begun to look outside our circles for a compliant girl, someone yet unformed. She was struck by your potential. She shooed away the maids and fussed over your ankle herself. My brother coaxed your phone number out of you and my mother insisted I inform your family of your state because it was only proper that I call your home, not he. Once our families had exclaimed sufficient gratitude and claimed nothing but neighborly duty, it was understood that I would be your new best friend and my brother, your suitor.

Now here we are, in your rose-scented dressing room on your wedding day. You have no sisters, so I've had bestowed on me the honor of being both from the groom's side and the bride's. I had fretted at first, revisiting every bilious memory of you flirting with him. What of the times when you and I sat back-to-back on my bed inscribing our journals until he wandered in and enticed you away with a bundle of bottle-green glass bangles? What of the secrets in those journals that we shied from sharing, but ravaged with stolen glances? What of the ache to be part of those secrets? And the time we fought, so you ran off and let him steal his first kiss from you? And then you crept back with chafed lips that I soothed with butter? What of the time we chose cut-silver nose studs for each other, you a crescent moon for me, and I a glinting star for you? Where do those moments bleed into what I am to do with you today?

But it has occurred to me that I will be preparing you to be brought into my home, too. You will be ensconced in what was previously my brother's cave but has lately been referred to as the bridal chamber. This means I bring not only you, but also your next life into mine.

So let us begin with your soul. We sift through your things, and I stay your hand as you reach for every trinket in sight. I cull away at your memories and harden your heart against all that was your past. You are allowed only a few protective charms: your rag doll that banished your nightmares, your journal that freed your tongue, and you may bring your little servant girl if you wish. I gather these items and take them away with me to arrange in your room-to-be.

Now your body: allow me to lavish your face and limbs with turmeric to illuminate your skin. Let me massage warm oil into your hair. Let us rinse away the flaking henna from your hands and feet and marvel at the filigree that adorns you. Here are the marigolds I will braid into your hair. I swathe you in red silk so laden with golden vines that you cannot move—which is just as well, since your strapping hero plans to carry you into your chamber in his arms.

Here, now you are settled on the bridal altar in the wedding tent. A cushion under your left arm, one last pin to tuck away the veil from your glowing face, and now I must leave your side and join the groom's procession.

IT IS LATE. WE HAVE BROUGHT YOU HOME. I watch him carry you into the chamber I have prepared with your things. I pace the cold marble of our veranda all night. When the sun rises will you walk out of that tomb? Or will it be the portal to your next life?

Telling Tales

Dubai, 1989

Anyway, the scandal of it all was lost on me. The mirror had seen everything, and all of it was true, every tale already known in our hearts. I, like countless others, had come to Dubai on the wings of our relatives' dreams; and sometimes, to escape the web of nightmares they spun around us. We came with papers but no plan.

As our sights cleared like the morning haze lifting off desert wadis, revealing an unrelenting bone-dry landscape, we saw how our permits were in fact shackles. We woke each sunrise to our employers' demands and ran after sundown to neon-lit money exchanges to wire home the dirham bills crushed in our fists.

At the salon where I worked, after hearing my name called so often in one day that my mind lifted away from the sound of "Shireen," I steered the body-that-was-Shireen the way I wielded a mop. I thought of Hajar who ran back and forth between the desolate peaks of Safa and Marwa to find a drop of sustenance for her wailing infant. How abysmal her search must have felt; how hellacious it must have been to keep faith in salvation to come, to see a purpose in her abandonment by the father of her son,

God's own prophet who believed in a bigger design; how the only thing that kept her from succumbing to a suicidal stillness must have been the fact of her parched child. I, my sister's keeper, tried, but in the end, I did not know if I had Hajar's strength.

How many of us did? It was no wonder then how easy it was for our own truths to put a crack in our midst. Shatter our bonds. Send us careening to alight on other soils. Some of us found it in ourselves to root anew. Others were lost to the sands.

The mirror I want to tell you about was mounted in the back panel of a clawfoot china cabinet that sat in the henna room of my salon, witness to hours of gossip from every part of town, and even abroad. The application of henna requires a repose of the body, every stroke liable to smudge, leave an indelible error in a woman's adornment. So, tongues ran instead. The thing about Dubai in those days was that no one imagined an end. They told stories with abandon, as if nothing could come back to haunt them. But the mirror saw everything and had nowhere to unburden itself of all the knowing that seeped into it: cross-border intrigues, neighborly infidelity, the momentous, the petty.

The china cabinet had come to the salon by way of Mrs. Alawi, the sister of our most demanding patron Mrs. Suleiman, both women loyal clients despite our humble location. They had installed in the salon, and trained to their needs, a waxing girl, a facials girl, a manicurist, a hairdresser, a makeup artist, and yours truly, a henna girl. Their deal with Sobia, the owner, was that they would pay our salaries as long as we were available to them at no charge the minute they walked into the salon. Our little alley in Deira was treasured by these sisters because others in their circle were not likely to wander to this part of the city and discover the talent they had nurtured. Of course, they had no need to think about what else the owner did with us girls.

I cleaned at night. I saw the games Sobia played—machinations so convoluted, she had to work them out along the straight lines of notebooks. She recorded half of our salaries from the sisters as a tip, which she held on to for end-of-year-bonuses. Who lasted a year with her? And she put us to work on every other conceivable chore and more. She earned double on us and gave us half of what the sister-patrons paid. Sometimes these chores involved accompanying certain customers home, as temporary day help. Sometimes the customers dropped us off and their supposed-husbands were home, and no one else. If your heart is racing for us girls, know that we survived; and in the end, that's what matters. We adjusted. One does when one has to.

I did. Because I had run with Noreen after my father, in another one of his rages, smothered our mother with her own pillow and threw her in the river that cut through our town. I dragged Noreen, six years younger than me, and ran barefoot with her to my grandfather's house. The next night our mother's sister Ghazala, who had only been visiting from Dubai, prepared the bloated body for burial. Ghazala Khala had to scold Noreen to stop the hopscotch game she had begun with other children on pillows from the funeral prayer room. Our grandfather told Ghazala Khala she must take us in. Clearly, we needed a woman's hand. He, a rich widower with an open drinking habit and famed gambling ways, lived a life not predictable enough for young girls. He promised her money to keep us.

She had a little boy of her own. She had only wanted Noreen, who was already charming with her tiny, upturned nose, and was sharper than a knife even at the age of nine. But our grandfather knew I had seen things only I could protect Noreen from. To convince Ghazala Khala, he also promised his house to her husband Fazal-ur-Rahman, who was a teacher at a sham private school in Dubai that helped students cheat on their board exams.

Ghazala Khala had me help her with the housework after school, and the day I turned eighteen, finagled me a work visa for Sobia's salon so I could supplement Fazal-ur-Rehman's earnings. He mostly sat smoking at a snack shop around the corner from the salon, waiting for his number to be called up in the US green card lottery. In fact, as he sat there, he argued with everyone else to apply for it as well. Night after night, as I helped Ghazala Khala make rotis for dinner, she complained about how the man, a farce of a math teacher, couldn't fathom that every new Pakistani application reduced his own chances.

If I was too tired from the salon to help her, she would make the rotis herself because she had decided that Noreen was going to live the dreams neither she nor I had been able to. She wanted Noreen to study; she wanted Noreen's hands to remain soft. She treated her like the daughter she had wished for after she had been fortunate enough to have a son as her first born. Her pride in Noreen was second only to her pride in her boy Haroon. "He takes after our side of the family, you know," she'd tell me as she hovered over the smoking tawa, burnt flour in our nostrils. "Never raises his voice. And look at his handsome face. Just like your grandfather's." Every week, she made me wash my little cousin's laundry by hand, along with my little sister's, while the children did homework together. I soon offered to do the whole family's laundry, and she took that time to supplement her husband's earnings by tutoring Mrs. Alawi's children.

And that was how the mirror first came to the cramped courtyard villa we rented. Ghazala Khala had been teaching the children in Mrs. Alawi's drawing room where the cabinet stood when, with a little creak, a plate from Mrs. Alawi's gold rimmed wedding dinner set slipped off its half-shelf as if it had been tipped off. Bone china shrapnel shredded Mrs. Alawi's fingers as she, in an inexplicable furor, swept the cabinet clean with her bare hands. "Please," she begged Ghazala Khala, "please, take it from me. Take it to your house."

At home, some premonition tugging at the base of my neck, I warned Ghazala Khala not to accept it even as she asked her husband to hire a couple of day laborers for the move. "It's odd that she would give away such an expensive piece of furniture, don't you think, Khala?"

"I'm doing her a favor, really," Ghazala Khala said. But she couldn't resist acquiring a piece of home décor that her acquaintances had not even seen in the markets.

And so, that night, two wiry men sweated on our doorstep as they fought the cabinet. Their trousers rolled up, their feet slipping and sliding in dusty sandals, they yelled at each other in Bengali as the cabinet tipped this way and that—stubbornly, newly heavy on the side opposite to the one they'd just managed to support with unnatural postures. As they finally cleared the doorway, the mirror on the back wall of the cabinet creaked out a complaint like a cat being dragged against its will.

Khala, something about that screech disturbing her, had the cabinet placed in the room Noreen and I shared. "We'll figure out where to put it later," she said, and offered the men some strong chai in addition to their pay.

How many nights I watched the mirror on the back of that cabinet while Noreen slept the peaceful sleep of those who have labored with their minds all day, their bodies able to find tranquility instead of fighting aches. In the daytime, you see, the surface of the mirror is compelled by the brightness of the outer world to reflect us back to ourselves. But a mirror has depth. On its inner wall fall the shadows of the world the surface soaks in. This mirror, I found, held on to its shadows like filmic memories instead of giving them up like the ghosts of the day, as you would think mirrors must. My personal memories weighed on my own soul, tore holes in its fabric. So I was not surprised to observe that this mirror was already sagging with its burdens in the wooden notches that framed it—you could see the strain of its weight on the holds at the bottom, cracks beginning to snake in their grain; you could see the gap the mirror left at the top, the millimeters it had already slipped. I wondered how many memories it took to drag the mirror down one millimeter; if different memories had different weights.

After staring at it for weeks, I began to recognize two shadows. A female shape I knew well, and one of a man. The woman was one of our sister-patrons, Mrs. Suleiman. I did not recognize the man. But they were doing things to each other I cannot speak of on Mrs. Alawi's sofa. I knew that sofa from the times Mrs. Alawi had asked me to babysit her children when her English nanny took her paid vacation twice a year.

There were other shadows too, some more faded than others, and they played over each other like faint black and white movies projected on a single cinema screen. I wondered about the mirror's scream as it was forced into our house. What was it resisting? Were new rooms heavier to record? It was a tired scream, I decided.

I was tempted to whisper to the mirror every detail of how my father had dragged my mother by her hair and then forced himself upon her even as he smothered her. I had seen it from the corner of their closet where I had hidden with Noreen. I had held her head to my chest and cupped her ears closed and so she only remembers the heaving of my chest, the wet of my tears down her head. Maybe if I finally spoke of what only I had seen, the mirror would take it from me, and I would be unburdened. But I recalled the desperate plea in the screech of the mirror. I couldn't burden the tortured thing with any more than it was already tasked to hold. I thought once of hanging a curtain over the cabinet, to give the mirror some relief. Then I thought, would I rather have been blind than seen what my father did to my mother? Instead, I began to wipe the glass front of the cabinet with vinegar and newspaper. If the mirror could see, let it have clarity.

Months later, despite my warnings, Ghazala Khala had the cabinet moved to the dining room. She could not, finally, resist showing it off to her visitors. She tried once to budge it herself, but she was no match for the claws that dug into our bedroom carpet. On an impulse, she recruited a visitor her husband had been nagging her to invite for dinner—some young gardener called Fazal he pitied to no end because he was his name-sake and had grave visa troubles that were the talk of the chai shop. As a recompense for feeding him, she had Fazal help her husband drag the rattling cabinet to a side wall in the dining room, a place of pride across from her end of the table. She couldn't understand why I objected, and even accused me of being greedy. How could I tell her about the ghosts I had seen? The ghosts that, I was now sure, had driven Mrs. Alawi mad.

I didn't have to wait long for Khala to discover what I had. After sending us all to bed, she had a ritual of sitting at the table with a quiet cup of green tea. She beckoned me out of bed one night, a finger on her lips. I crept out, my quilt around my shoulders, and pulled a chair to her side of the dining table as she directed me to. The air conditioner hummed to a stop just as I began to discern in the mirror, faintly, our bedroom. How had I not seen this before? I'd been concentrating so hard on the well-established shadows, that I hadn't noticed a gauzy new one forming. But once I recognized it, I could not unsee it. My room. The bed Noreen and I shared. Noreen, undressed. Noreen touching herself. Everywhere.

Ghazala Khala sniffed up tears. She took such a big sip of tea that she choked and fell into a coughing fit. Fazal-ur-Rehman rushed out of their room and she screamed at him to leave her be and return immediately to bed. The man did as he was told. Haroon peeked out of a small crack in the door of his room, but then shut it when his mother began scolding his father. He'd always been terrified of her raised voice. Noreen, who slept the unburdened sleep of those who've sold off all their horses at market, didn't even stir. The door to our room remained closed the way I had left it.

When Khala and I were alone again, she took my hand and calmed herself with three deep breaths. "Shireen," she said, searching my eyes, "tell me the truth. Have you taught her these things?"

I yanked my hand away and backed away toward the kitchen. "No," I said. "And do not imagine such a thing about me again." I had never been rude to her before. But she had no idea the things I had protected Noreen from. Yes, the acts of our father upon our mother. But also the acts that had been visited upon me more than once. Acts I had swallowed so deep, I hid them even from myself, or I would not be able to return to the world the next day, to the life I had promised I would negotiate so Noreen and I would always have a roof over our heads.

"She has to leave my house," Khala said. "Next, she'll be ruining my boy."

Something about the loneliness I had seen in Noreen's shadow broke the walls I had built around my ego for the last few years. I fell to my knees in front of Khala. "She's about to graduate high school," I said. "Please, let her finish. I'll help her do those tests for foreign colleges. I've heard other girls talk about them when they come to the salon with their mothers. If she can't make her way elsewhere, I'll take her back to Pakistan myself."

Ghazala Khala relented. Still, the next evening, she called Haroon into the kitchen where she and I were preparing dinner and forbade him, in front of me, from spending any more time with Noreen than was formally necessary at home. He met my eyes questioningly, but I maintained an apathetic expression, and he was old enough to know that there were things women saw that men just had to accept the spirit of. It was all drama on Khala's part anyway—Noreen had stopped playing with Haroon a long time ago because she was popular at school, and he was two years younger.

But Ghazala Khala was not done with her precautions. She came to the salon with me the next morning and appealed to Sobia's cheapness, convincing her in minutes to accept an intricately carved mirrored cabinet with rare claw feet. By the salon entrance, once the cabinet had been safely installed, she said to me, "Don't worry, the salon is closed at night. Nobody will see anything."

I nodded and smoothed with my hands the shredded paint on the salon's door frame from where the claw feet had held on as the Bengali movers, now the only ones Khala trusted to safely get the thing out of her house, shoved the cabinet through the opening that would have been wide enough but for the feet that caught. One of them suggested sawing off the feet but I screamed no as if they had been talking about my own hands. Khala and Sobia looked at me oddly. "Can we have it in the henna room?" I'd asked, to distract them.

And that was how it came to be that every night, as I cleaned up after my last client, I massaged the ache from the claw feet with a soothing cloth soaked in hair oil. The mirror was leaving more and more room at the top of its framing, much faster than before, so I knew it was getting heavier, the feet in pain as they held up the shadows that accumulated in the mirror. There were uncountable stories told in that room every day. Sometimes I stayed long after the cleaning was done to watch the new shadows. They sat still, their palms up. But their heads, their mouths moved along with their tellings.

They commiserated about aunts beaten and sisters deserted. They gleefully cheered hurried weddings that they would later denounce outside those walls. They spoke of how their friends tricked their husbands and fathers, they spoke of their husbands' sleights of hand in business deals. In fact, Mrs. Alawi, whose husband was in the Emirati foreign service, spoke of trouble between the Pakistani president and his wife. Mrs. Alawi happened to be in the company of an American dignitary's wife, who she'd brought to the salon for an authentic henna application. She did not know that the cabinet had been adopted by the salon, but could not react, nor leave because she had brought a guest.

The American woman, who had not expected the process to last so long, and had sipped too much of the champagne that Sobia had sourced just for her, spoke of how an upcoming American arms demonstration to the Pakistani president and his army chiefs would probably not go too well. But, she insisted, Mrs. Alawi was to keep this between women because if the word got out, the men would cause diplomatic destruction of unprecedent proportions.

"And that's why they need their wives," Mrs. Alawi quipped back, "to hold their little secrets." The two women laughed then in a way that held more stories than the one just hinted at.

"Oh shush," the American said. "Now tell me, how's your beautiful sister, the one married to that dashing head of that bank?"

Mrs. Alawi downed her friend's champagne and said, "May my sister burn in hell."

Both women snorted out their drink in a laughing fit. A stray line of henna trailed down the American's arm. Mrs. Alawi glared at me.

"No, no, not her fault," the woman said, wiping off the henna with her hand and then gaping at her stained arm in horror before letting me do the wiping with my tissues and towels. The women spoke of dealings I could not comprehend in my exhaustion and because I did not know the worlds they spoke of.

They considered waiting at the salon while the henna dried. But the mirror creaked so loudly they were startled out of their floor cushions. Everyone else had left by then. The three of us stared at the cabinet because it was as if it had called for help. And then I noticed one of the back claw feet buckle and the cabinet tip down in that corner. I ran to steady it. Mrs. Alawi and her friend fretted and offered to help prop it up.

"Take care of your henna," I said. They were frozen. I looked up at the rosewood clock, the only authentic thing in the salon, to check if time had stopped. The clock carried on. "Leave!" I yelled to shake them awake. Mrs. Alawi came back to reality at my insolence and frowned. I begged her then, "Leave me to it." I had to be alone with the cabinet in that moment I had known would come.

As the door closed behind them, the brass bell tinkling wildly with the hurry in their exit, the other back foot cracked and then split. The cabinet slammed to the floor on its back side. The mirror, jerked violently in its housing, so pregnant now with its burdens, broke its casing and toppled forward.

And then it was all glass and mirrors inside that cabinet. I stayed by the side of the thing, holding it up. As the rosewood clock ticked away, the effort it took to brace the cabinet lessened. As it became lighter, I slid to the floor, leaning against it as it gave up its ghosts.

Tales must be like cats, with a compass for home. How many stories can I tell you about the next day? Three or four you might care about perhaps.

Noreen confronted Ghazala Khala about her recent attitude, and when the woman coldly told her what she knew, Noreen told her all the things she could do with her own body that her husband wouldn't, which led to Ghazala Khala dragging her to the airport the same day and putting her on a plane back to Lahore with the pay money she had been safe-keeping for me. Mrs. Suleiman visited her sister in a frenzy of honesty and repentance, begging for forgiveness, but Mrs. Alawi walked out of her own house and left her husband a note that Ghazala could keep an eye on the children's education and the maids could feed them, and he could find solace in her sister any time he wished. Right after an arms demonstration by the Americans, General Zia-ul-Haq died in a plane crash along with all his men, and also some big Americans—which told me someone in DC or London or Dubai was suddenly very unhappy about something they'd learned, but I don't know much about such things.

Fazal, the gardener who had been on the run from Mrs. Suleiman's husband of late, was outed to the authorities by someone at the snack shop and thrown in jail for three months before a scheduled deportation back to Pakistan. Fazal-ur-Rehman consoled himself about the whole thing by telling Ghazala Khala not to fret about the boy since he had convinced him to apply for the green card lottery. Ghazala Khala took to her bed with a scarf tied tight around her head at this news. "You think they're going to let in two Fazals from Pakistan?" she yelled at her husband, who'd followed her to the door of their bedroom.

Huma—I haven't told you about this girl because I was complicit in the hiding of her—she, too, had been seen by the mirror. Mrs. Suleiman had concealed Huma, her maid, at the salon. She'd hidden her from her violent husband's wrath for some infraction so grave that she feared for the girl's life and not only her job. Here Huma cleaned the bathrooms and floors and dusted at night because Sobia fired the cleaning girl as soon as she received Huma from Mrs. Suleiman. On the day of revelations, when secrets took wing like angels of retribution, condemning those who would turn their eyes from them, and freeing those who would acknowledge them, Huma tired of living in concealment and emerged from the janitor's closet to the shock of a client having her hair bleached. She extracted airfare from Sobia on the spot by threatening to reveal to Mrs. Suleiman all she knew about how she ran her business, and with the help of some travel agent she knew took the first flight that day to a Pakistani airport. It turned out to be one to Lahore where she knew nobody but could swear freely in the streets to get what she needed and find her way home.

And I—I opened in the quiet of my bedroom the jewelry box I'd brought home the night the mirror broke. At the salon, I'd dumped out of it Sobia's plastic gems and fake gold, and laid inside it the two unbroken claw feet and the largest remaining shard of the mirror before walking home through the night streets of Deira, silent but for a passing taxi, cooler without the heat of the bodies from around the world that ran the city's machinery all day, bright with the marquees of every business run by the sweat of an outsider who'd coming looking for some kind of luck. I knew I would not return to the salon in the morning. It was like blood had been spilled there.

Nothing, you see, nothing was truly a surprise to anyone who was confronted with what the mirror had witnessed. Scandal was a charade we had put on. In my room, where Noreen still slept for the last time, the shard of mirror glinted back cheerfully at me. I watched it all night but saw no shadows in it. It was like a newborn babe.

Mrs. T Receives a Gift

LAHORE, 2017

Mrs. Tarar—who was known to have been a grateful child, then a dutiful wife, and now a contented mother—found herself one October morning unable to stand up from the chair at her dressing table. She had donned a freshly pressed shalwar kameez, wriggled on the sapphire rings Tarar Sahib had gifted her at the births of their two sons, and clasped on the generations-old lapis lazuli and gold bead necklace handed down to her with much ceremony by her mother-in-law. Then, after some consideration, she slid on a new platinum bracelet her older son Asim had sent all the way from New Haven.

Mrs. Tarar hoped the bracelet might provide a tolerable topic of conversation with which to break the silence with her husband. They had parted in an unfortunate manner at tea the previous day. For the first time in their marriage, she had been the one to walk away. The light of day sparkling through her pristine windowpanes made her think she might have acted petty. She was anxious about the embarrassment she had caused her husband in front of the household staff—and in front of his mother.

Though she hated to upset the cook's plans, she determined to look into the breakfast preparations and request Tarar Sahib's favorite fenugreek potatoes. As head of the staff, the cook would have myriad outlets to express his frustration in some clandestine way later that day, but so be it.

As she pushed down on the brocade chair to get up, she discovered that her lower body was lead.

"Pari!" she yelled out to her personal maid. "Pari?"

Several footsteps thumped down the corridors toward Mrs. Tarar's bedroom. Parveen flew in. The cook and the laundry girl halted in the doorway.

Parveen panted. "What…happened…Iram Baji? Sorry…Missitea?"

"Get me out of this cursed chair, Pari." Mrs. Tarar bristled at the idea that she sounded helpless. At forty-five, she felt as fine as she had at thirty-five. She'd just seen her younger son, Yasir, off to college and felt as if she could raise another. She was assiduous about her health regimen, with long walks and plenty of greens, lemon, and turmeric in her diet, so she wouldn't flesh out like her mother or turn arthritic like her mother-in-law.

Parveen grasped Mrs. Tarar's arm and pulled—to no avail. She grabbed both arms and yanked, but only managed to fall backwards. "What a day for you to be stricken like this," she moaned from the floor.

The laundry girl shuffled, then blurted, "Didn't I tell you all? This new foreign name is a bad omen. First Sahib ji and now—"

The cook glowered at her. "Watch your mouth. Can't you see Madam—Missitea—is in distress?"

Mrs. Tarar smacked the arm of her chair. "I didn't ask any of you to call me that!"

"Sahib ji's orders, no?" the laundry girl quipped, then ducked under the cook's raised hand and dashed down the hall.

TWO MONTHS AGO, AS MRS. TARAR returned from Lahore airport after seeing Yasir off on his flight to Houston, she had looked forward to curling up in her quilt in the silent darkness of her room with her own thoughts. There had not been a day in the last twenty-five years that she had neither son at home. As the chauffeur drove them back, she kept her gaze on the streets, unable to engage with Tarar Sahib's chatter.

As they pulled up at home, an assembly of familiar cars blocked access to their carport.

Tarar Sahib laughed. "You see, I knew you would need distraction today, so I've asked all our dear friends over for dinner."

At Mrs. Tarar's distraught look, he added, "Cook and Parveen have this under control. You don't have a thing to worry about." He watched her face until she attempted a smile and then, satisfied, exited the car to embrace his best friend, Dr. Rafiq, who had also just arrived.

As dinner led into dessert, Tarar Sahib, settling in with his cup of chai, polled the gathered company for their opinions on how his wife might deal with her inevitable doldrums. "It will be a few years yet before she can expect the blessing of grandchildren to occupy her. It seems our elder one, Asim, is busy with all that, but in no hurry to settle down. You know how it is in America."

The men chuckled. The women, several of whom were already satisfied grandmothers, eyed Mrs. Tarar with sympathy. She averted her eyes from them and got up to make sure that the elder Begum Tarar, her mother-in-law, got her chai the way she liked it—half-a-cupful with extra milk and one stevia tablet. Begum Tarar was hard of hearing, so her son rarely bothered to ask her opinion, though in Mrs. Tarar's experience, she had plenty to say. She particularly enjoyed ordering Parveen about, despite having the laundry girl at her disposal in the months that she stayed with them. Tarar Sahib had instructed the entire household to attend to his mother's every need.

"Maybe Yasir will keep an eye on Asim," Dr. Rafiq said. He slurped his tea.

Tarar Sahib popped an entire rasgulla into his mouth. "That younger boy of mine doesn't know his pen from his…" The rest of his words were lost behind the napkin he used to wipe the syrup from his mouth. "I'd hoped his cousin, Zeeshan, might show him the ropes, but my wife here won't let him live with my sister. She's not wrong though. The boy needs to develop some independence."

The men talked over each other boisterously, sharing jokes about their own ignorant youths, and some who'd known others since their schooldays brought up unsavory memories, then cut each other off with, "Come on yaar, the ladies, think of the ladies."

Mrs. Tarar did not like the way Tarar Sahib had spoken about her studious Yasir, the way Asim might have about his younger brother. She felt an unfamiliar urge to leave her husband's side. For over a quarter of a century of marriage to Tarar Sahib, who was ten years her senior, she'd preserved her sense of dignity by acting with honor. Too many eyes, including the present company, had waited to see an inexperienced girl slip, undermine her husband who already had a significant social standing in the community, thanks to his inheritance and a savvy ruthlessness.

At his invitation, Tarar Sahib's guests pondered Mrs. Tarar's options, bandying possibilities back and forth like a shuttlecock in a game of badminton. They cheered Dr. Rafiq's shot.

Dr. Rafiq, on the slightest encouragement, would bring up how his wife, as the long-time principal of a private elementary school, had raised the school's rank to the number one spot among the elite families of Lahore. "No one can escape her sharp eye or her iron fist—not the students, not the teachers, not even the parents."

Not even her husband, Mrs. Tarar thought he might as well add.

Mrs. Rafiq neither opposed, nor confirmed her husband's reportage of her success.

Mrs. Tarar understood how she saw no point in interfering with her husband's joy. Of all of Tarar Sahib's friends' wives, Mrs. Rafiq had been the most cordial after her wedding, advising her on how to interview help, and who to mix with. However, Mrs. Tarar had been too young, and Mrs. Rafiq too busy raising three children, for them to nurture a friendship.

"Theoretically," Dr. Rafiq explained to the group, "she can create a new administrative post at the school to offer our sister."

Mrs. Rafiq maintained a blank expression, so Mrs. Tarar knew that Dr. Rafiq's enthusiasm would remain in the realm of theory.

Begum Tarar clanked her teacup down on its saucer. "Respectable," she exclaimed. "The house of Tarar has always been respectable." Mrs. Tarar got up to clear away the teacup. No telling how much her mother-in-law had heard. Her outburst could be perceived as a rebuttal to Dr. Rafiq, but, just as likely, it could have been a demand to remove the dirty cup from her sight. Or, she might have objected to the men's earlier banter. Begum Tarar's proclamations were often delayed.

However, Tarar Sahib's face assumed a concerned expression. "Now, Rafiq, not any position will do."

Dr. Rafiq patted his comrade's knee and turned to his wife. "We understand, don't we?"

Mrs. Tarar knew that a positive reaction was expected from Mrs. Rafiq, so she gave her an excuse. She made eye contact with her and smiled broadly. Mrs. Rafiq smiled back. The room was gratified. Mr. Tarar moved on to ask his friends' opinion on how he might handle a troublesome constituency in a provincial district he'd held for over twenty-five years. Pleasant camaraderie over the lamentable state of national politics carried the rest of the evening.

As Mrs. Tarar had predicted, Dr. Rafiq overestimated his wife's ability to create an administrative post at will. Several weeks after the party, the best Mrs. Rafiq managed was to bring to their attention an opening for a kindergarten teacher. Still, Mrs. Tarar found herself intrigued by the prospect.

In the weeks since Yasir's departure, she'd felt lighter not having to worry about his needs hour-to-hour. But she carried some guilt about this; missed talking with him. Asim had grown distant as soon as he hit puberty, but Yasir would do his homework by her even through high school, chat about the novels from his literature class—many that she read for the first time along with him, amazed that only a decade ago, she had been teaching him to read. She imagined reading stories with young children again.

"Do you think we should consider it?" she asked Tarar Sahib over breakfast. She looked at her toast, and not directly at him, because she did not often make requests that involved only her interest.

At first, Tarar Sahib dismissed the idea altogether. He told her he'd learned that the opportunity had already been placed in the papers. "I can't have my wife competing with riffraff."

After Tarar Sahib left for a tour of one of his pharmaceutical factories, Mrs. Tarar gathered her courage and called Mrs. Rafiq at the school. On hearing Tarar Sahib's objection, Mrs. Rafiq offered to Mrs. Tarar that, if she chose to apply, she would be the first interviewee on the list.

At home that night, Tarar Sahib reconsidered the suggestion, given the development. "I'll have a talk with Rafiq," he said. He ate his dinner in uncustomary silence. "It's an absurd little job, wouldn't you agree? How much can they pay you?" He scooped the last of the kofta curry from his plate with a piece of naan and chewed thoughtfully. "Not that you need the money."

"It's not the pay," Mrs. Tarar had hardly touched her naan as she awaited further objections from Tarar Sahib. "I thought it might be interesting."

Tarar Sahib laughed. "Do I bore you? You'd rather keep the company of children."

"You're not always home—"

"I can be, you know." He took the hem of her dupatta and rolled it between his fingers.

Mrs. Tarar glanced around for the servants, embarrassed. "It's different," she tried, then in her hurry to change the subject, brought up money again even as she regretted it. "Even if the paycheck is small, it would be fun to earn something for once. I'll give it away in charity if you like."

"What I like is for you to be there when I'm home." He observed her untouched food. "I had worried that I'd lose you to depression. But now it seems your mind might be elsewhere."

Mrs. Tarar took a few bites of food to set her husband at ease as she considered her next move. "Would we be disappointing Dr. Rafiq—after everything?"

Tarar Sahib sighed. "Fine. I need to call him anyway. An issue with his last order turned up at the factory today."

The morning after her interview, Mrs. Tarar received a phone call from Mrs. Rafiq. Given that the school year had already begun when the previous teacher had resigned, the school board decided that despite Mrs. Tarar's lack of experience, because she spoke well, had raised two boys successfully, and could start immediately, they would offer her the position. Before she hung up, Mrs. Rafiq mentioned, as an aside, that several board members were pleased at the prospect of listing Mr. and Mrs. Tarar's name on the school's promotional materials.

That night Mrs. Tarar tossed in bed, chafing about Mrs. Rafiq's last words. As dawn broke, she determined to pour her heart into the work and prove herself worthy of her position.

After her first week of teaching, Mrs. Tarar returned home exhausted but glowing. Never had so many persons clamored for her attention and appreciated the effort she put in all day. And how they loved to hear a story! She set up her class day to begin with story time and end with a reading too.

Friday was a half-day, so, as soon as she arrived home, she hurried to her room to freshen up for a quick tea with her husband, and then to head out with the chauffeur to acquire supplies to convert the reading nook in her room into a workspace.

But when she entered her bedroom that adjoined Tarar Sahib's, she spotted on her dresser an unfamiliar box amidst the usual jumble of mismatched candles. She preferred to think of the candles as Tarar Sahib's. He liked to make love by candlelight. She had become known among their friends for her passion for collecting candles. People gifted her artisan candles made by destitute women in far-flung villages. They remembered her when they vacationed in foreign countries. She accepted their gifts grudgingly. Tarar Sahib would visit her through a low interior door between their bedrooms, choose a candle, make love to her in the shadows it threw, and then blow it out as he left her bed. Receiving these candles embarrassed her. It felt as if the whole world were complicit in the rhythms of Tarar Sahib's visits to her room.

The box that lay by the candles that afternoon was a matte-black cube. At first, she thought it might be another gift of jewelry from Tarar Sahib. If they ever had a disagreement, he made up for it with a gift. But they had not seen each other enough this week to have disagreed on anything. In fact, today would be the first time all week that they'd be having afternoon tea together. She smiled at the possibility that he might have missed her. But then she shook the thought from her head. Years of missed teas had gone by without note as he stayed out on factory tours and political engagements.

The box on the dresser was of a sleek, more modern style, heftier and colder than the ones Tarar Sahib chose. She opened the magnetic flap of the lid and peered in. A wide platinum cuff bracelet caught the light in its fine hexagonal mesh carving. She lifted the beehive of a bracelet with one finger and marveled at its weight. Mrs. Tarar noticed tucked inside the box a paper note. She unfolded it cautiously, worried it might be a receipt forgotten inside by the careless gift-giver. It took her a moment to recognize Asim's handwriting. He had made the effort to use a fountain pen.

Darling Mama, I got this for you from my first paycheck. I want you to know that your son is now in the proud position of being able to take care of you forever.

Her heart plummeted even though Asim had probably expected it to leap. Her own paycheck was not enough to sustain her lifestyle, but it had felt like a portal. She would never speak of it, but she had even looked into what kind of housing she might be able to rent with it. Just as a joke, not a practical curiosity. Asim's words felt like she had been found out, like a pinprick in some childish balloon. She reread his last words and let the note drop. She retreated from the room without stopping to change.

In the living room, Begum Tarar, already ensconced in her armchair with the antique lace doilies, prayed under her breath on the amber beads of her tasbih. Tarar Sahib waved Mrs. Tarar to the sofa chair next to his. "Come, come. How lucky we are today to have the pleasure of your company."

She recomposed herself and smiled. He could have been talking about himself and his mother, but Mrs. Tarar knew that right then he was referring to himself in the old-fashioned collective first person. This meant either an occasion for displeasure or humor. She did not have the verve to deal with either. "And I, yours," she mumbled.

"The school must be keeping you terribly distracted." He wiggled his right eyebrow in the way he used to indicate he was only half-joking but was willing to accept the situation he had chosen to jest about. "Now tell us." He settled back in his cushions with apparent relish. "What has been your favorite part of the week?"

"Well, the children have taken to calling me Mrs. T." She relaxed at the memory of how it began as they begged for one more story the other morning.

This set Tarar Sahib off into a belly laugh. "That's all?" he asked.

In their time together, that laugh had been a consolation to Mrs. Tarar that her husband, though much older than her in years, was not like those dour, under-confident young men her cousins had wedded. By the time of their marriage, Tarar Sahib had already established a reputation for big-heartedness toward those who moved in his circles. If Mrs. Tarar ever scolded him gently for being overly zealous in his gifts, especially to his friends in government posts, he distracted her with a box of barfi from the best sweet shop in town, or if he had been objectionably extravagant, a sparkling jewel for her. Such had been the rhythms of their nominal disagreements because Mrs. Tarar had learned quickly to not interfere in his domains. The children and household, he left to her, as long as his mother did not complain. The content Tarar Sahib never failed to announce at his annual get-together with his old college mates that no man in this city ("not a single man," they had begun to chant after him) had made a better match than he.

But when Mr. Tarar laughed about the children's nickname for her, Mrs. Tarar suspected that perhaps he had laughed at her and not with her. Disturbed by Asim's gift, and now, frustrated with her husband's jocular manner when she should have found it pleasurable, her sense of confusion escalated.

Her frustration must have reflected on her face because Mr. Tarar stopped mid-laugh and watched her for a few seconds. She did not make small talk to lighten the silence. He struggled out of the sofa (his knees had been troubling him of late) and went into his own bedroom where he rustled about for a few minutes. When he emerged, Mrs. Tarar spied from where she sat that he was hiding something behind him. Instead of returning to the drawing room where tea would arrive shortly, he ambled down the hall toward the kitchen. His presence in the kitchen was such a rare event that Mrs. Tarar anticipated the tumbling of pots and the skittering of maids that ensued. He then returned to the drawing room empty-handed and lowered himself into the sofa again.

Tea was brought in, not by one of the kitchen girls, but by the cook himself. After he had unloaded the serving tray, the cook composed himself and, with a flourish, reached for the tea cozy.

"Stop," Tarar Sahib said. The cook's hand froze above the knitted bobble of the tea cozy. "Where are the others? Call them all in. Our task has grown."

"Let him pour my tea first!" his mother chided.

Tarar Sahib said, "Ji, Ma," but flicked his finger at the cook to do as he had asked.

The others Tarar Sahib summoned comprised the battalion of household help. They came in from their various stations around the house and grounds and formed a knot by the beaded curtain at the entrance. Once the gardener had thumped his four-year-old nephew to stop him from chewing on the beads and everyone was paying attention, Tarar Sahib nodded at the cook.

Mrs. Tarar and Begum Tarar watched as the tea cozy was lifted to reveal a carved wooden box.

"What's wrong with you?" Begum Tarar scolded the cook, having expected a teapot.

Mrs. Tarar understood the box was meant for her, that it would be velvet-lined (Tarar Sahib never used cheap boxes), but she couldn't guess what might be nestled in there. He was beaming with anticipation, so she obliged him by reaching for the box. She brought it to her lap, but as her fingers hovered over the lid, he said once more, "Stop."

She stayed her hand and suppressed a sigh.

He turned to the company at the threshold and proclaimed, "The lady of the house would prefer to be called 'Mrs. T' and we have gathered you here to let you know that we expect you to humor this wish from now on."

The gardener's nephew asked the laundry girl the meaning of "Missitea," and was poked into silence by his uncle.

Mrs. T waited until Tarar Sahib nodded at her to proceed. As she unlatched the lid, a tight bundle of rupees that had been suffocating inside the box gasped out onto her lap. Tarar Sahib leaned back in his chair, pleased with the drama enacted by the bills. Mrs. T regathered the money, including some that had spilled to the floor, and looked toward him with the blank face she reserved for those moments when she wasn't sure what expression would best gratify him.

"Three years of teaching salary," Tarar Sahib announced. Then he glanced around the room as if they were in an auditorium. "Now our Mrs. T has her name," he elevated his voice, "as well as the money she will have no need to toil for."

Mrs. T's gut curled as tightly as the notes that had been tucked into the box. There had never been a need for expressions of gratitude between husband and wife. So, when she got up from her chair without a word, Tarar Sahib did not lose his smile.

She walked over to the servants with the cash in her hand. They parted to let her pass. She stopped by the gardener's nephew and told the boy to show her his hand.

"I swear, Missitea, I haven't taken anything," the boy said. He wouldn't meet her eyes and instead scowled at his uncle, his hands clenched.

"Do what Madam…Missitea says," the cook barked.

Mrs. T waited for the boy to comply even as her head felt hazy. Her soul was determined on an act that her mind seemed powerless to resist. The gardener pried one of the boy's grubby hands open. Mrs. T placed the wad of rupees in the boy's hand, closed his fingers over it amidst gasps from the other servants, and walked off to her own bedroom. Her mind wrestled with the act even after it was done, and finally retreated, boxing it up as charity.

Tarar Sahib had not called her back, or enquired after her at dinnertime. He had not entered her room at night through the little door. So she prepared to face him the next morning and endure whatever form his displeasure might descend in, most likely an extended absence to tour the family's rural estates without her, or worse, late nights out with Dr. Rafiq on what they called cultural shows—lewd dances, in Mrs. Rafiq's opinion, that defiled the history of the art form with suggestive lyrics and moves imported from cinema.

But the next morning, when she had steeled herself to leave her room, she had to first contend with the clutch of her chair.

Parveen made a third attempt to free her, this time grabbing her under the arms, but it was as if a boulder had been placed on Mrs. T's lap.

"Oh, what a day for this catastrophe," Parveen whined again.

"I'm not doing this on purpose, Pari," Mrs. T snapped.

"But Missitea," Parveen said, looking back and forth between her and the cook. "After you left, Sahib ji was holding his chest and wouldn't let any of us near him, not even Begum sahiba. He sat there until dinner time but would not eat. Cook had to help him into bed."

Mrs. Tarar panicked on the inside but maintained her composure so as not to alarm the staff. "Has anyone checked on him this morning?"

"He won't let us pull aside the curtains," the cook said.

Parveen leaned in and whispered, "He's been asking for you as he comes in and out of consciousness."

"For me?" Mrs. T whispered back, her eyes wide. He had never asked for her before. He never had need too; she had always, somehow, been there. She glanced at the private door between their rooms. Tarar Sahib used that door whenever he wished to visit her at night. She only ever had need to enter his room via the main door off the hallway to check on whether it had been tidied properly. Sometimes she brought him his paper if she hadn't seen him in a day and wondered if he was home or had left on a last-minute trip without informing her.

Mrs. T appreciated Parveen's speaking discreetly of his request for her. If Tarar Sahib were in his full faculties, he would not have expressed a need for her in such a vulnerable manner. She must answer his call secretly; she would use the inner door to his room. Given his state, she decided that news of the bracelet from Asim would not be appropriate, so she removed it.

No sooner had she slid it off than she felt as if her chair, too, had loosened its hold on her. She shifted and found that she could move again. She stood up, unsure what had just occurred, but was relieved to rise to her full height.

"It seems that I'm alright," she told Parveen in a low voice. "Leave now—I'll see for myself what he needs."

Alone again, she approached the door between their rooms and considered it awhile. But she could not bring herself to proceed before investigating something more pressing in her own room. She turned back.

At a groan from the other side of the wall—her husband's voice, yet strange to her ears—Mrs. T hurried to the little door and nudged it to peek in. Tarar Sahib's room was dark and dank. She maneuvered around his bedroom slippers and a newspaper that had slid off his bedside table. She squinted as she approached his slumped form. She dared not pull aside a curtain or turn on a lamp for fear of shocking his senses. Her foot landed in a damp patch of carpet. She jumped back at the thought that she might have stepped in urine. But a ceramic soup bowl lay on its side nearby. Begum Tarar must have ordered the bleary-eyed cook to brew a batch of chicken broth at the crack of dawn and tried to press it on Tarar Sahib. The broth was probably resentfully under-seasoned. The room smelled gamey.

Tarar Sahib turned to her, his face as pale and gray as the newspaper clippings that hung framed on the walls of his room—local news stories about his business conquests and political coups.

Surprised by a sensation of revulsion, Mrs. T paused. She had expected to feel pity, not disdain. "What's wrong, Abid?"

Her husband emitted a pained grunt.

"You need water." She searched the room to see if anyone had thought to bring in a pitcher. "I'll call Dr. Rafiq."

She picked up the soup bowl and opened the door to the hallway, but Tarar Sahib called her back. Reluctantly, she shut the door. He was struggling to sit up, so she helped him, tucked his hair back from his forehead and propped him up on his pillows.

"You don't need us, Iram—we see." He attempted a smile.

Mrs. T sat at the edge of the bed and watched her husband of twenty-eight years. *But you have always needed us*, she thought. She took his hand and put off the call to Dr. Rafiq until his breathing settled and he fell into a peaceful sleep.

DR. RAFIQ WAS UNABLE TO IDENTIFY what ailed his friend. Mrs. Rafiq proclaimed, in a rare voluble moment, that it looked for all the world like a broken heart, and how wonderful to know that Tarar Sahib had had a heart all along. She offered Mrs. T as much leave as needed. Apparently, she had no shortage of substitutes.

In the two short weeks that followed, no one expressed surprise at the forbearance Mrs. T exhibited as she saw Tarar Sahib through his pain management, and then his last rites. Hers was the shoulder everyone leaned on: Begum Tarar (despite accusing Mrs. T of having given her son a heart attack, which she believed had been corroborated by Mrs. Rafiq); their sons (Asim had flown back on emergency leave, but

Mrs. T had insisted Yasir not return so as not to jeopardize his student visa); even Tarar Sahib's business colleagues (who needed a sign on whether to initiate certain deals that had been agreed upon and Mrs. T instructed them to carry on in their best judgement, because one must).

Tarar Sahib's sister called from Houston. "Will you be okay, Iram?"

They had been best friends before they were made sisters. The fluid ease of their girlhood relationship had not survived the strain of Iram's earnest commitment to her role as a married woman. At the sound of Zeba's voice, Iram almost buckled under a craving to be held by one who knew her. But she had trained herself out of that need for too many years now. Put oceans between that need and herself. She had mastered the art of distraction. She changed the subject to talk of their boys.

Over those days, Mrs. Rafiq told Mrs. T that it was in such trying times a woman discovers her might. For her own part, Mrs. T found the obligation in that time no different from what she had done all these years. Just as she had fulfilled her duties as a wife to Tarar Sahib in life, so she did in his sickness and death.

But it was after the funeral that people were confounded to see no change in her manner. She did miss his cheer, found herself unmoored not having to anticipate his every need. But there was much to be taken care of. She had never been one to buckle to what was past, had a way of seizing the present.

Mrs. Rafiq told her that she had tapped into a supernatural reserve of strength during her husband's illness. She could use time to recover. She suggested that the substitute teacher might be offered a permanent position and Mrs. T need not return to teach after her forty-day mourning period. Mrs. T accepted. Both women knew that the House of Tarar needed her.

Mrs. T sent Asim back to New Haven, surprising him with a gift of the sapphire she had worn in his name every day, telling him the ring would probably be of better use to a new generation. She considered keeping Yasir's ring, but then, at the airport, sent it on to him in Asim's care. She convinced her mother-in-law to return to Tarar Sahib's younger brother's home. There she would have grandchildren to fuss over. As she tucked Begum Tarar into the backseat of the car with a warm blanket, Mrs. T handed her the lapis lazuli necklace, saying that it would be more appropriate worn by the wife of her living son. Begum Tarar could not argue with this, but her astute eyes lingered on the neckline of Mrs. T's newly tailored tunic. "The lace shows well against your complexion."

After Begum Tarar had departed, Mrs. T asked Parveen to accompany her to a jewelry store to replace the silver star of her nose stud with a diamond of her own choosing. On the way back, she stopped at her beauty parlor and asked the hairdresser to give her an appropriate look for the various business meetings that were pending on Tarar Sahib's schedule. She knew that she would have to pretend to understand the finer points of the discussions until she developed a sense for them. But she would have to endure, because it would have deeply concerned Tarar Sahib to think that people who had expectations from him had been disappointed in any way. Their sons had no interest in the details of their father's businesses, though they had inherited substantial gains from it. Mrs. T thought she owed it to Tarar Sahib's legacy to receive the people who still had business with him.

First, the creditors came, and when she had dispensed with their business, they stayed for tea. Word spread that the House of Tarar was still welcoming guests, and the creditors were soon followed by the usual stream of beggars, both financial and social. When she took refuge in her brocade chair from all this coming and going, Mrs. T realized that she was the only one who was not amazed by her fortitude.

However, she remembered with clarity her own moment of surprise.

After Parveen left her room on the morning of Tarar Sahib's sickness, Mrs. T had turned back from the door to her husband's room because of a nagging thought. Back at the dressing table she picked up the platinum cuff bracelet from her son. She passed it from hand to hand, feeling its carvings, marveling at its weight. With a deep breath, she sat down on her chair and slipped it on. The force that held her down again crept up from her legs into her gut. She felt it tug on the back of her neck, on every nerve now. She shook off the bracelet with such force that it clanged against her mirror, cracking it. And she found that she could stand again.

She reread the note in the box. The pang of dread she had felt on the discovery of the bracelet the previous evening returned. She crumpled the paper. Her next instinct was to tear it up, but the thought felt like a violation of maternal mores. So she gave in to the impulse in a controlled manner and tore off just a little corner. A brief sense of release pervaded her at the fulfillment of this act. Still, she could not bring herself to tear up the whole note. She placed the paper and its torn corner in the box. She set the bracelet on top of the note and chose a half-used candle from her bedside. She lit it and buried the note in a pool of translucent wax. The bracelet, too, was glued to the bottom of the box. This gave her such relief that she chose a heftier candle, wedged it in the middle of the bracelet and lit it. The candle dripped its wax slowly into the gift box as she headed for the door to Tarar Sahib's room.

Mrs. T returned to her room all day to ensure the flame in the box remained lit until the entire bracelet stood buried in wax.

Rotis

Dubai, 1990

I leave for college in New York next month so my sister, Shireen Apa, has decided I should be taught the essentials of survival. We've had mend-your-clothes-by-hand day. How-to-dissuade-a-man day. How-to-disable-a-man day. How-to-treat-wounds. How-to-disappear. How-to-resurface.

Today is how-to-make-rotis day.

"I know," Apa says, "I know, it sounds old fashioned, Noreen. But, baby sister, there is a hunger as deep as a well in people like us; one that only a flaky roti right off a hot tawa will satisfy."

She takes great care not to make me think she wants me to be a housewife. She isn't one herself. She manages a bustling salon in the heart of old Dubai. But it's an unspoken hope amongst the working girls here: a life of respect.

Apa has aspirations of a professional future for me, higher even than I dare imagine. She holds me responsible only for the state of our bedroom and my desk, because, presumably, a clutter-free environment is important for my studies. She insists we house with the other salon workers so we can save for my college, all three of the other girls in one room and Apa and me in the other. Nana, our grandfather, forced me back from Lahore to finish school here, unable to keep me because he had no home, had lost it in a game of poker of all things. *I have nothing to teach you*, he'd said.

Since I returned to Dubai, I've managed to evade this airless fifty-square-foot kitchen. Battered pans from four different countries totter in a stack: the Filipina's kawali, the Sri Lankan's chatty, the Bengalan's hari, Apa's karahi. They're all round pots for God's sake, but each girl simply must have the one her mother used. They've come to look exactly alike, the grease stains on their outsides from the same colossal can of sunflower oil we pitch in for. The pantry is choked with communal dried milk containers rattling with beans and reused jam jars stained with the pigment of spices. I've learned to shut up about the creak of the cobwebbed exhaust fan because the girls all feed me, somehow of one mind that I should get the higher education they never could. I also shut up about the midnight cockroach on the floor drain, the sunrise lizard on the single sooty window.

Nana threw me back on Shireen Apa who'd been too spineless to defend me against our aunt, that old prude Ghazala who'd accused me of lasciviousness when Apa and I lived with her, and sent me back to Pakistan even though I was almost done with high school. But Nana assured me my return to Dubai would pass like a storm does; he told me to be patient and not offend the fortune that came my way. *Make use of it*, he said. *Your aunt, your sister, they're steppingstones. Your mother had all your potential, Noreen, but not your luck.*

Nana had always loved our mother more than his older daughter, Ghazala. I was only nine when our mother died—she'd been screaming at our father again that day. Next thing I knew, Shireen Apa forced me into a cupboard full of moth-bitten clothes and then dragged me through our empty cottage and ran with me all the way to Nana's house. No one has told me how our mother died, though I've always known not to look for our father. They say he ran away that day.

What if he ran from grief? What if he was lonely without his wife and daughters? *He's dead to the family*, they told me. And then news came recently, in the short time I just spent with Nana, that our father had finally died—taking a new wife and their infant daughter with him, leading them far down a train track outside the dusty town they lived in, tying them both down and throwing himself on top of them. That is the act of a broken man. Maybe I could have saved him—if they'd let me look for him all these years. But I'll never know.

So, I look now only to my own future, as Nana has told me to. No one understood my father. No one will understand me. I wait by the pocked aluminum tray we use for kneading our various daily breads.

Apa drags the jumbo sack of flour from the pantry. Reaching above the stove, she tugs the string on the exhaust fan. It dangles uncomfortably high for her. I could reach it, but why bother with something she does every day anyway. I steel myself for the smoke that will soon invade my nostrils because that fan is a flop.

"Stone-ground wheat is the best," Apa tells me. "God knows what you'll find in America, though."

I jiggle the flour she's measured out in a sieve positioned over the aluminum basin. I imitate the wrist movements she shows me; still, a fine powder spills over the sides.

"Keep going," she says. "Will you believe what our mother said when she was teaching me? The chaff will make your roti ragged, and then who will marry you?"

She brings me a cup of hot water from the sink. "Work in the hottest water your fingers can bear," she says. When I wince at the heat, she winces too. She reaches as if she might mix in the water for me, but then pulls back, telling me instead, "Our mother used to say the hotter the water the softer the roti, so the scald will be worth it."

When I manage to pull together the first crumbs of a dough, she tells me to gather them and knead. "With a determined fist," she reminds me, over and over again. Then, with a gentle touch on my clenched hands, she stills me. "Give it time now," she says. "Let it relax its fibers." We wait together, my eyes on the dough, her eyes on me. "Our mother told me how, after such a beating, rest makes dough pliable. She warned me to remember this." I know the wait might be at least half an hour. I'd never wondered what Apa did in that half hour every day. "I've thought about her words on this matter," Apa carries on, her eyes faraway. "It was years before I understood why she called it a trick."

We reminisce about the games we used to play with our mother's pots and cooking utensils; the bites of our own food we secreted away in our dupattas for our dolls' weddings. Usually, our mother scolded us for that. But the day before we ran, the day before she died, she had helped us sew new dresses for our dolls. From a torn kameez of hers. I was surprised at the rips in that kameez—it was a new one she'd recently sewn. I think to ask Apa about that kameez as we wait. But then I decide I don't want to know. It's been too long.

We make a dozen balls of dough together. "Tear off only what will fit in your hand," Apa warns, showing me. "More will only be trouble, our mother used to say."

We don't call her "Ammi" like we used to when we were small. For years we didn't speak to each other about her, and others referred to her as "your mother." Later, she simply became "our mother." That way, we stopped pining for the times we could speak with her.

Apa motions for me to bring the rolling board and pin from the rack above the counter. She sprinkles some loose flour on the board and hands me a dough ball. "Okay, roll it into a perfect circle," she says and chuckles when I throw her a look of betrayal. "The first time I made rotis," she says, "our mother said to me the circle must be perfect. Here, you are on your own." Apa added a nasal tone to that last line, which takes me aback. It is our mother's voice; one I had forgotten the sound of.

I flatten and roll out the dough with too much care and not enough pressure. Apa leaves me to my attempts and strikes a match. She lights an open flame, and then another one under the griddle.

"When the tawa is hot enough," she says, "lay your roti on."

"How hot?" I ask.

"Throw on a pinch of flour. It should toast, but not scorch."

She hovers a palm over the tawa for a few seconds, then nods. I drop my crude disc onto the griddle.

"When the first side blisters, flip it and let the other side cook, but only barely."

As the second side of my roti turns opaque, Apa is on her toes. "This is your moment—flick the roti onto the open fire."

For a fleeting moment, I'm on the verge of tears, terrified of failure, convinced the flame will spitefully turn to ashes the half-done bread I've smothered it with.

But then, the layers of my roti begin to flake. They rise up with the breath of the kitchen, ballooning the roti right up to its spherical edges.

Apa lifts my roti off the flame with her bare hands and places it in my open palms. "Our mother used to say," she says, making me look her in the eye, "if you've done everything right, you'll hold the world in your hands. Do not let it burn."

Bungalow

Houston, 2020

At the bottom of a street marked "No Outlet," in front of the pocket-sized bungalow to which I'd summoned my realtor on a whim—okay, a notification from the realty app—I leaned on my car in a perfunctory pose, pretending to scroll through my phone. The realtor had warned me about rash decisions, especially in flood-prone Houston. Under the search criteria he'd helped me set up—concerned that as a twenty-something with a solid down payment in hand but a dodgy understanding of the housing market, I was a flighty case—this house would have been filtered out. But I had two searches. One to match his. One to browse in the bathtub.

This listing had only one picture—the front of the very cottage I used to draw as a child, dreamed of as a teenager as I tossed on a foam mattress my itinerant mother had unrolled for us on the floor of some new room we'd borrowed, a blazing streetlight stabbing my eyes through another curtainless window. I stood now in front of a bona fide white picket fence, a porch with a cheery swing, a front door pat in the center, equidistant windows hugged by shutters, kissed by white azaleas already abloom in February.

The realtor's car coasted up to mine. Striding up to me, eyes on his phone, he reappraised the write-up of the property. "Says here," he looked up to make sure I was listening, "says here, as-is. You understand?"

I nodded; dutifully surveyed the particulars as well so he couldn't accuse me, when I would shortly insist on pursuing the property, of being deluded. The description comprised a terse history of long-ago improvements, clipped factoids in passive voice. A land-value investment; a tear-down. Not a word about the fence gate with the carved ducklings. Padlocked now. A laughable impediment—I could simply hop over the two-foot barrier.

"You don't want to break any conditions of the sale." The realtor knew by now my disregard for red tape, my affinity for loopholes.

"Just to see what the swing feels like?" I jiggled the gate lightly, perhaps expecting the padlock to fall off the way an enchanted doorway must open for the one predestined to enter.

The realtor shook his head. He pointed out the buckling beams straining to hold up the porch, the tilting windows neither parallel to the door nor to each other, the towering willow smothering the roof and likely worrying the foundation. The realtor dealt in houses, not homes. He was legalese embodied. Realtor, a fitting title.

But as a mathematician, unknowns did not daunt me; risk was estimable, precision a distraction, the truth better discerned with an abstract eye. And the truth was, I'd promised myself just such a house as a seventeen-year-old the day my widowed mother took a taxi to the airport and flew back to Lahore. She had buckled in her attempts to survive in this land her husband had brought her to as a young bride and then left her to falter in without an education, without an income, without ties.

"I need to be somewhere my feet know the earth." My mother's last words to me were more than a plea for understanding; they were a mutual acknowledgment. I, too, was choosing to part with her, to stay in the city of my birth rather than flounder in her unlucky shadow, news of which seemed to precede us, close doors we hadn't even approached.

As a child, I dreamed of a daily breakfast table straight out of the sitcoms I devoured at school friends' homes—checkered tablecloth, one sunny-side up egg, buttered toast, a tumbler of orange juice. My mother would rather save face than eat.

Every time she had fallen, it was because she had waited on someone else for passage, for shelter, for love. My mother was a good woman with a fickle fate, her sense of dignity her demon.

I admired her. I would not be her.

I agreed to let Haroon, a high school teacher, the only real friend I'd known my mother to make, help me run the bareboned Hillcroft coffeeshop she left in my hands, let him check on my safety in the rooms I slept in above the shop because he lived in an apartment across the street. Teacher, I called him teasingly in those days because he used to tutor me in math so he would have an excuse to visit with my mother with whom I was sure he was in love. Teacher, he remained to me after my mother left; a simple man, faithful to a fault, torn for two whole years between caring for me and his crabby old mother, Ghazala Amma, who'd held some inexplicable grudge against me back then, almost as if she were jealous, even as she sent over home-cooked food for me every weekend. When I moved to San Antonio for college, I'd missed her cooking as much as I'd missed Teacher.

If I felt at all guilty about taking this step, it was that Haroon would be disappointed I had not consulted him. He'd recently helped me sell to eager commercial developers the coffeeshop property I eventually inherited. My mother, on her return to Lahore, had sought out the owner of the building—a man twice her age who had let her use the abandoned property as a favor to her parents. She'd ingratiated herself with him, then married the man and persuaded him to bequeath the property to me. For the first time in her life, she'd compromised. But not on her own account.

I should have been grateful. I was disillusioned. Felt unfettered with no one left to simultaneously idolize and reject. Felt, finally, orphaned.

Teacher disagreed with me. Tried to tell me that love took many forms. I told him the love songs he listened to were out of fashion. That was the only time we'd fought.

The least I could do to alleviate his concern about my new house was to be able to tell him I'd considered the state of the neighboring properties. The place across the street, in a minus one on that count, appeared to be condemned, peeling neon orange and green notices posted on windows invaded by tentacles of ivy. But, and I told myself, more significantly, the place next door looked identical to this one and was immaculately kept.

On the twin bungalow's porch sat a person hunched over the *Chronicle*, an incalculably old woman with a mutinous mop of silver curls. She'd been peeking over the paper at me from the moment I'd stepped out of my car. If she could thrive in her house, surely, I could manage in its twin. Plus one. I considered myself even.

"One bed, one bath. Only eight hundred and seventy square feet." Realtor was readying his arguments.

"Perfect," I said. I wanted a home I could learn, a space I could fashion.

"You can afford a new construction condo in Rice Military for the same asking price. We've discussed how this Heights market is too hot for its own good."

"I don't want a condo. I want a home." The realtor sighed, so I added, "A house. This one."

He huffed, agreed to send in the offer within the hour and headed to his car shaking his head, a bit dramatically I thought. It didn't matter. I was the one generating *his* paycheck. Though I did need him on my side until closing, so I turned toward my car as if I too were done. But as soon as he cleared the corner, I swung back to the padlocked gate.

A creak from down the sidewalk checked me. The Ancient next door was shambling out of her fence gate. Hands in the pockets of a quilted pyramid dress worn over frayed jeans, she came up and joined me in observing the cottage.

"Gonna take it, kid?" Her voice was whiskey, Leonard Cohen an octave higher.

"It's yours?"

"My sister's. She died. Lived here alone, but we had each other." She looked me over. "You got somebody?"

I shook my head. Wondered if Akeli, my tabby, counted. Haroon was somebody, I supposed, but he never hovered. Work was what I woke up to, running risk management models for oil and gas companies all day. My laptop came to bed with me, to catch up on emails from the team. Lovers rarely lingered, and lonely as I was, I compartmentalized, carried on with my degrees until a year-long relationship in grad school. But he moved back to California, and in the end, I couldn't picture wandering out West, beautiful as he was. For months, I missed tracing the curve of his spine with my fingers, the charge as he traced mine with his lips. But

I relished being able to dream my own dreams again. I was volunteering at a pet shelter in those days and found myself unable to tear away from a five-month-old skittish underweight kitten abandoned by callous owners. I was warned that she'd been taken from her mother too soon, she'd had no house training, she'd been deprived of nurture, she ate indiscriminately and pissed on everything. Maybe it was the void my boyfriend had left in his wake, maybe I understood her; I decided it was her and me. We would make a home together, civilize each other.

"Wanna see inside?" the Ancient asked.

"What about terms of sale and all that?" I asked, somewhat unnerved by her interest in me.

"It's sold. Tell 'em I told you."

"Wait, it's not leaching poison or something, is it?" Even as I accused her of trickery, I was ashamed of myself. "How did your sister die?"

"Wandered too much, if you ask me. Fell off a cliff last year, hiking to her last day." She scrunched her eyes at me. "You hike?"

I shook my head.

"There you go, you'll be fine."

Never had I felt so welcome before. I extended my hand. "I'm Zoya."

She took mine in both of hers—knotty-veined brown hands that held the wisdom of tree bark. "Billie."

The weekend after closing, I invited Teacher over to help paint my porch, to make him feel included. I lugged home one too many gallons of buoyant yellow, something cheap pre-mixed off a Home Depot shelf because I figured that, as a homeowner, I hadn't yet earned the right to splurge. To my disappointment, Haroon said Ghazala Amma was so unwell that he couldn't leave her alone all day. I should have gone right away to see her. Not for her; for him. But I found myself unable to return to that drag of a neighborhood so soon after embarking on this new life. I commenced painting on my own.

I'd moved in the very day Realtor had slid the wee manila envelope of keys toward me, tucked his half of the commission into the breast pocket of his pilling navy blazer and relayed to me a relieved congratulations. I unrolled a foam mattress onto the floor of my empty bedroom. The irony was not lost on me. On the first day, Akeli laid claim to the floor of the pantry. By the second weekend, I developed a dry cough, a slight nausea that was worse by bedtime.

It had to be a problem with the home. I hated to admit it. I was better at work. There, I looked up symptoms instead of running the crude oil futures models my clients were waiting on. Google pointed to some invisible problem, likely mold behind the walls, maybe dander in the HVAC, possibly radon under the floor.

Haroon came over two weeks later on a blue Vespa, two long rectangular boxes roped to the back. I'd sent him a picture of the house. He'd brought me a housewarming gift: bamboo shades for my front windows.

He did a slow three-sixty around the house, hands clasped behind his back, raising an eyebrow at every crack. He'd taken to wearing an avuncular moustache in the manner of the Pakistani singers of yore I'd seen on the covers of the CDs he'd bring over to play for my mother. I followed him around like a kid in trouble. To my relief, the house sensed the gravity of the moment and behaved better as well. The floorboards hushed their creaking under Teacher's steps, and the windows drew in a cross breeze that freshened up the interior with the scent of gardenias that had burst into bloom just that morning.

He admired the view of the backyard from my bedroom window. "You have space to build a sunroom out here. How your mother loved the Houston winter sun."

Refusing a precarious seat on the porch swing, he settled on a step with a glass of homemade lemonade I'd spruced up with mint and a pinch of salt, the way I'd seen his mother do when she wanted to spoil him. He set the drink down without a sip. "Have you read the inspection report carefully?"

I stifled an oncoming cough and nodded. There hadn't been a pre-sale inspection because of the as-is clause.

I'd simply wanted this bungalow with its sagging porch that I would sip my morning coffee on until it fell under me, and then I'd get up, dust myself off and figure out how to rebuild a porch. In the back, I had hung bird feeders from the redbud and elm, and tamed the underbrush with Billie's weed whacker. After dinner at the table-slash-prep-surface tucked under the kitchen window, I took a cup of tea to the clawfoot porcelain bathtub whose eggshell enamel was cracked on the outside as if the bird had just hatched. I sat in bubbles until I got wrinkly, then curled up with Akeli in my twin-sized bed. I'd been delighted to discover that the bedroom could only fit miniature furniture—a dolls' room with no one's whimsy to consider but my own. I had stumbled on the small bedroom set at a garage sale two blocks down. It came with a letter-writing desk just big enough for my laptop. The only upgrade I made to the house was to install wiring for highspeed internet access. I didn't have the heart to get rid of the landline and ethernet sockets, which looked like orifices innate to the structure, and even left hanging a yellowing old ethernet dongle, now daily prey for Akeli. The house had, so far, turned out to be the tractable space I'd expected, necessary and sufficient for the life I wanted, not one that was a remainder of my mother's fractured dreams, nor a construct of Haroon's hopes for me.

I had decided that living in a space was an act of daily inspection. So, despite the realtor's stern advice, there had been no post-sale inspection either. Hence, I concluded, my wordless affirmative to Teacher's query was vacuously true.

As Haroon eyed me suspiciously, Billie arrived at the fence gate and seeming to decide the visitor was okay, came on in without stopping to ask if it was a good time. It was as if the place was still her sister's.

"Not your father, I suppose?" she said to me.

Haroon cleared his throat. I could have relieved him. Described how we'd met. But I was curious to see what he would say about who we were to each other. He'd never been much of a talker. I poured Billie some lemonade.

"She's like a daughter to me," Haroon told Billie finally. He looked down at his shoes, but then looked up at me pointedly. I'd made him recall my mother. I looked away, regretting having pained him, and introduced him to Billie.

"Our girl here might be dying a slow death," Billie told Haroon. "That cough? Carbon monoxide, I say." She thumped the porch beam triumphantly, knocking off some flaking paint. "A slow, sneaky leak somewhere. Has to be. Folks across the street?" She pointed at the condemned house. "Old man began to hack, then talked looney for months before it got figured." She looked right into Haroon's alarmed eyes. "Aren't you glad I remembered?"

Teacher jumped up and sniffed the air, then crept to the front door nose first. "Call the fire department, Zoya," he said between sniffs.

I watched testily from the threshold of my own house. Akeli dashed from corner to corner to dodge his feet. When she flattened herself to crawl under the sofa, I scooped her up and shooed him back out. "You're scaring Akeli!" I yelled.

"What an inauspicious name!" Haroon scolded back. "Why would you call her 'lonely?'

I'd meant "lone," not "lonely." Same word, big difference. Akeli's name had been aspirational, wish fulfilment, a chant, a note to self that no one else would become my point of failure—a hex against my mother's mistakes. How to explain this to Teacher?

"Are you planning on dying on her in this place?" He was more worried about the state of the house, about my prospects in this home than I'd expected. He was seeing omens in a cat. It wasn't like him.

"You sound like Ghazala Amma," I snapped. I used to think she was a superstitious old witch and suspected she'd driven my mother away, though I wouldn't have been able to say how.

It was as if I'd slapped him. He watched my face for a long minute and said, "How would you know what she sounds like now?"

He stepped off the porch, glowered at Billie as if this whole turn in my life had been her fault, and scootered away. My middle went hollow. His lemonade sweated into a moldy crack in the decking. What had I wanted from Teacher? Not help. A blessing, perhaps. I didn't think I believed in signs. But still, he'd left me without one.

"Now listen to me, kid." Billie patted my arm. "I'm not leaving here till you make that call to the fire department. That he was right about."

"I don't want to make a fuss for nothing, Billie." I couldn't imagine a single other person scrutinizing my house that day, giving me check marks, telling me whether or not I could make this my home. I promised I'd look up the non-emergency number and saw Billie back to her place.

Billie plopped down on her porch rocker and continued to watch my place. An hour later, the exact scenario I'd feared unfolded.

A siren tore up our street; a fire engine as large as my house now stood wailing outside my gate. The Ancient must have called 9-1-1 for me because I didn't know better.

My neck hot with embarrassment, I rushed up to explain. But the firemen had already hopped the fence. They bounded up the porch. They raced around the house. Six men, all of whom, I could have sworn, were twenty-one years old and seven feet tall. Three of them wielded crowbars and pickaxes. A stout six-footer with a well-trimmed moustache brought up the rearguard. The guys asked him for directions with a "sir," and he instructed them with a "son."

"No one is in danger of dying," I told Sir. "Really. I just need to make sure there isn't a tiny carbon monoxide leak somewhere."

Sir nodded at a lithe firefighter with curly dark hair who yanked a meter off his belt and yelled something at the others. They huddled behind him to enter my home, then paused en masse when the low doorframe slammed his head. Slowing down, each of them ducked and were admitted one at a time. I followed the pod, watching them squeeze through doorways like fluid via an inlet and explode into the next room, crowbars held close, meters sweeping every nook.

Curls noticed my distress and broke off from the others. He nodded toward the porch. Out there, he asked me, "Do you have an attic, ma'am?"

His quieter voice was a surprise to me, a relief. I'd expected the tone he'd used with the guys. Instead of responding, I shuffled the paint supplies to one corner. I was stalling in my response to Curls. One, because I'd never looked for an attic. Would he think me foolish for not knowing this about my own house? I wasn't the kind of person who needed an attic, who boxed up past lives and lugged them around. And two, despite my anxiety about what was transpiring, I hadn't been able to look away from him, the way he moved with a panther-like power. Before I could expose myself, another one of my coughing fits compelled me to sit down on the swing.

Curls watched me with concern, then turned the gallon of paint with his boot. He shook his head. "You should be wearing a mask with this. You shouldn't have this in the first place—there's way better ones. This here," he said, snapping the lid on the bucket with a thump of his fist on my cheery yellow and edging it to a corner far away from me, "is your problem."

I shook my head, still not fully recovered.

"It is," he said.

Sir barked out a summons, declared an all-clear. Curls spun around, the corner of the swing scraping his shin with a vengeance. He trooped out with the other firefighters who appeared collectively hyped to have determined that the situation was under control. Sir told me to call 9-1-1 if I smelled anything.

Curls paused at the fence gate as I followed to close it. He made as if to tip his hat, but he wasn't wearing one. Maybe it was a salute. I wasn't sure. Didn't look like he was either.

"Good luck," he said. "You can always—"

"Call 9-1-1," I finished for him. "Yup, thanks."

"Look, if you really want to use that paint, get a mask, or better yet, get someone else."

Whatever those fumes had done to my lungs, they probably did worse to my good sense. I heard myself saying, "Like who? You?"

Curls looked over at the guys who'd been loading up the truck. He shrugged and jogged back to his team. I stepped out behind them and strode over to Billie who was still watching from her porch.

"Why would you do that, Billie? It was nothing after all!"

"Well thank the Lord," she said with a grin. "If they'd found something at yours, they'd be over at my place next."

"So that's it? You weren't worried about me dying after all."

Billie's smile withered. She got up, looking worn. From her front door she asked me, "Why is it only this thing or only that thing with you?"

I'd managed to be ungracious to both Teacher and the Ancient in the same day. I'd cheated on my house; I'd plied it with lousy paint, then almost invited a stranger to slather it on.

I promised myself that I'd go buy the best paint next weekend, a cozy mustard perhaps, and not just for the porch. I'd treat the house to the chirpiest trim on the street, cinnamon brown maybe. I'd get new frosted glass for the front door, ask for advice on all this from the local hardware store. They were a hundred years old, knew these homes inside out, and I was ready for them to adopt me, show me how to breathe life into the bones of my home.

The following Saturday afternoon I began again on the porch, first laying a coat over the area I'd desecrated with the other paint. At a creak from the fence gate, I spun around to see Curls. "Oh, hi!"

He came over gingerly as I stood in my splattered overalls, paint brush still in hand. He stopped on the bottom step, a bunch of sunny daisies in hand. I was eye to eye with him then and saw how easy it would be to know him. He was in a linen button-down with the rolled-up sleeves; he didn't look twenty-one anymore. He looked like he worked on his car on Saturday mornings and drove his grandma, who probably lived with him, to church on Sundays. I smiled.

He held the flowers out. "They match you. I mean…your beams."

I took the flowers to relieve him. If I didn't ask his name, I'd end up calling him Curls to his face. "I'm Zoya," I said.

"Carlos," he told me.

Close enough. I invited him in for a bite of kheer. "I make some every weekend to take over to Billie next door," I chattered on in my awkwardness. "She loves it. It's my mom's rice pudding." I was jarred by the sound of "mom" from my own mouth. In the years since she'd left, we were at first too poor to make international phone calls to each other, and then had grown too far apart to traverse the distance with voice. I hadn't called her anything in years.

I reminded Carlos to watch his head as he followed me in. The loose threshold bar tripped him instead. Akeli was curled in deep sleep on my two-seater couch, so, no living room for him. I led him out the kitchen door and onto the back deck. I'd thrown a weatherproof cover on the old foam mattress, to lounge on in the open air. There we sat cross-legged. He savored the kheer and sipped the chai I made to go with it.

When he told me his other job was as an Occupational Safety and Health consultant, I changed the subject, afraid of coming back to the topic of the paint, of opening my home, my homemaking, to his scrutiny, his insights. My house was an unsolved puzzle in the palm of my hand, one that I had an instinct for.

I spoke before he could, answered questions he had not asked: talked too much. He listened. But as the sun set and the cicadas awoke, I quieted. He met my eye, still attentive. A half smile played on his lips. It wasn't only his questions I'd been evading, but also the charge I felt from his proximity. As he took his leave, he left an ache in me, a sensation I had forgotten for too long now.

I waited to see if my craving would subside. When it only took on new dimensions with each day, my memory cannily extracting layers of meaning from every look, every touch of his, I asked him back next Sunday. This time he brought a bottle of rioja.

Saturday, I'd thought I'd check in with Billie, go see Haroon, his mother, who I'd learned had developed chronic laryngitis. But the shame of the things I'd said to Billie and Haroon, the regret over what I hadn't, seemed somehow, over the passing days, to have bloated into a dismal burden instead of dissipating. I imagined they were angrier with me now than they had been when we'd last spoken. As I filled up the day with chores for the house, eyeing every nook with the thought of Carlos' gaze, and then the sun set on the opportunity to tell them I had not meant my words, it dawned on me that this is what I had told myself about my mother over the years. My rationalization for not talking to them was a manifold sped-up version of my withered relationship with my mother. The truth was, Haroon had, my mother had, even Billie had helped me come into this home; each in their own way.

Summer wine sipped slowly leaves one hungry. Three luscious week-ends on my back porch with Carlos and I lowered my guard. Even as I suggested it, I knew I would regret it later. "Wanna cook dinner together?" I asked, before he spoke of leaving. I knew already how clumsy he was inside my house, as if every fixture stuck out a cheeky foot to trip him as he passed.

He squeezed into a chair at the kitchen table. There, he sliced onions, minced the ginger and garlic and crushed the tomatoes that I handed him for the channa masala we were throwing together. As we downed another bottle of wine, I made him name every spice in Spanish and left out of my recipe the things he couldn't name.

As the curry simmered, ready to give up its oil from the sauce, I squeezed past him as I had many times already to reach into the pantry for the garam masala, the final garnish. I then decided that he wouldn't have a word for garam masala anyway and hovered over him to inhale his scent.

We had to get out of the kitchen because, surely, Carlos said, one of us would catch on fire from the open flame we'd been kissing within a few feet of. Akeli had claimed the couch again, so I led him by the hand to the bedroom. We stopped outside the door, his hand tracing the belt of my jeans. We had to break our kiss to get through the low doorway. As I stepped aside to let him in ahead of me, a spark of panic lit up my gut. I couldn't tell if it was anticipation or anxiety.

At the sight of my dinky bed, he paused. Hand-in hand, we looked around my playhouse-sized room. He snorted, I giggled; we sat on the floor and laughed. I moved to my bed and he leaned against the wall in the nook by my desk.

"Sorry," he said, "maybe I've had too much wine?"

"No," I said, sober again, marveling at the effectiveness of my own armature. I had wanted no one else in this house. I had intended this as a bedroom for one. "This was the plan, I think."

He looked at me quizzically. "You're not stuck with this small room, you know." He rapped at the wall abutting the backyard. "We could knock this down easy."

How easily he'd slipped into the "we."

"It's fine," I said. Where could I begin describing the sunroom I had begun to plan?

"What is this place? Eight hundred or so?"

"Eight seventy," I informed him.

"It won't cost much. I could convince a buddy. It'd take two, three weekends tops."

He thought, perhaps, that I hadn't been able to afford more, manage more. "Dinner?" I asked instead.

I set Curls to warming tortillas on an open flame while I gathered the rest of the meal, then led him outside my home. He chose, for the first time, to try the swing. Fortunately, it was the chain that snapped at a rusty hinge—the roof of the porch and both beams held. Curls was on the ground, but at least the house was not yet ready to give up on me. I smugly considered texting Realtor.

Cross-legged on the floor of the porch, Carlos and I tore into the tortillas and scooped the channas with our fingers. The ideal space to entertain visitors, I decided. I wondered how I could fix up the outdoors to fit even more guests. I'd ask the Ancient for advice, how they'd entertained back in the day. I'd ask Teacher for his mother's recipes for a party. No, I'd ask her myself. For a minute I wondered what she might think of Billie. And then relaxed, certain that the Ancient could disarm even Ghazala.

As I latched the front gate behind Curls, I pulled my cell phone from my pocket. My mother's number sat in my favorites, never dialed from this device. Shama, it said. When had I switched from Mom to Shama? It would be nine AM in Lahore. I called her.

Acknowledgments

Thank you to my dear circle of writer-friends, some of whom have been with these stories for years and championed them when I faltered. Thank you, Elizabeth Cummins Muñoz who knows the soul of this book. Thank you, Lisa Wartenberg Velez, Hannah Kelly, Pritha Bhattacharyya, Stephanie Pushaw, and Nick Almeida with whom I began an almost impossible creative journey at the height of a pandemic. I kept my faith in my voice because of you. Thank you to all my other colleagues at the University of Houston Creative Writing Program. Each of you has touched this book in ways you might not even know.

Thank you Chitra Divakaruni for your mentorship, your inspiration. Thank you, Maurice Carlos Ruffin, Peter Turchi, Antonya Nelson, Brenda Peynado, and Robert Boswell for helping me see.

Thank you Inprint and the University of Houston Creative Writing Program for making it possible for me to have "a room of my own" with fellowships.

Several of these stories have appeared in a slightly different form in the following journals: A LEGAL ALIEN, *Fireside Journal*; A SHADE FOR THE WINDOW, *Cutleaf Journal*; LITTLE MOTHER, *Juxtaprose*; MAILEE AND THE SAINT OF HORSES, *Quarterly West*; MEHR, *Meridian*; TALKING WITH BOYS, *Witness Magazine*; TOP NANNY, SEASON 5, *AAWW's The Margins*. I am grateful to the editors of these literary journals. Thank you, in particular, to Areej Qureshi, whose words buoyed me as I titled this book.

Thank you to the Ahmed clan—my parents, my brothers—who have always believed in me. And finally, thank you to Rashed and Darius and Athena who are my home and my retreat.

author photo: Jamey Stillings

TAYYBA KANWAl is a Pakistani-American writer from Houston, TX. Her award-winning work has appeared in journals such as *Witness, Gulf Coast* and *Meridian*. Born in Lahore, Pakistan and raised in the United Arab Emirates, she holds an MFA from the University of Houston where she was an Inprint C. Glenn Cambor Fellow, and an MS from the University of Oregon. Her career has spanned technology consulting through nonprofit program management. She serves as Senior Editor at *Conjunctions*.